The Surrender of Julia
(Now and Forever 3)

by

Tammy Dennings Maggy

All inquiries should be addressed to the author at
www.authortammydenningsmaggy.com
Or
contact@sassyvixenpublishing,net

ISBN 13: 978-0-9913836-1-0
ISBN 10: 0991383613

Dedication

The Now and Forever series has been a labor of blood, sweat, and tears for the last three years. It goes without saying it's "my baby." The characters have become so near and dear to me that at times I find it hard to let them go after telling their stories. This is exactly the case with Julia Santos. She started out as just a brief mention in ***For the Love of Quinn*** in order to give background on Jacob Hartley. Now she has her own book. I couldn't let her go to fade into the background. She had a story to tell that shocked me at times. She's the villainess you want to hate, but at the same time you know there's something there worth redeeming.

Her story became so convoluted, I had to split it off from ***The Island (Now and Forever 2)***. It takes place the exact same time, but all from her point of view. Her story was too dark to have a home with Siren Bookstrand so her tale and those of the rest of the series will be with Sassy Vixen Publishing. I'll be forever grateful to Siren for taking a chance on an unknown author with a big dream. Because of their guidance and that of the fellow Siren authors, I found my voice and many more stories to tell.

I'd like to thank my fellow Seduced Muses for being there when I needed them the most and encouraging me to continue with my plans for the series. Maya DeLeina, May Water, and Nicole Morgan are three of the best partners I've ever had. You ROCK, ladies! Thank you for keeping me sane, allowing me to be as wild as I needed to be, and picking me up when I stumbled.

Lindsey Kirk/Bonnie Bliss, Amber Lea Easton, Stacey Jo Burns/Madison Sevier, and Natasha Blackstone, your friendships and guidance have been my rock and saving grace when I wanted to give up. Goddess knows those "give up" days hit me hard while getting this book ready for publication. Thank you for your shoulders to cry on, your ability to make me laugh when I just wanted to cry, and for just being yourselves. You're my sisters and I love you dearly.

To my fae, Tara Stevens Smith: every single day you show me that no matter what hell life throws at you, there's always hope. Your smiling face is what brought me through many dark days here twenty-five hundred miles away from you. Fate brought us together when we needed each other the most and now our hearts and souls will forever be intertwined. I love you my Moon Sister!

To all my friends, family and coworkers: thank you for putting up with my endless prattle about the characters yelling at me to tell their stories. You may've not understood why I have to keep writing, but you continue to encourage me to keep going.

To my husband Michael Liam Smith I owe my entire world. Without his love, guidance, and unwavering support over the last three years, I don't think I would ever write another word, let alone get it published. With him by my side we've created Sassy Vixen Publishing and a vision for a future that's oh so bright. He's my Knight in Shining Armor, my heart, my soul, my everything. The poem "Safe Harbor" that Julia and Carmen recite to each other is actually one I wrote for Liam before we were married. He is my beacon burning bright and always my safe harbor. I love you *mo anam cara*!

* * * *

Chapter 1

February 11th, Present Day, Los Angeles

"What if he doesn't want to see me after all this time? What if he can't ever forgive me for hurting him thirteen years ago?" Julia Santos continued to pace the floor of her art gallery as she wrung her hands together to keep from running them through her hair one more time. The new asymmetrical bob showed off her raven colored hair beautifully, but Julia had a hell of a time getting used to not having her locks piled on top of her head or cascading down her back. The new cut gave her a more professional and confident look for one of the biggest meetings of her career, but now her nerves were shot to hell and her confidence seemed to be fading fast. *I can't do this now. I should've never let Carmen send that letter to him.*

"Well, at least you tried. If you end up doing the artwork for the club at the MGM Grand, you may run into him from time to time. His brother *is* Stephen Eischer's right hand man. You're going to have to work fairly close with him too."

Julia stopped her pacing to stare at her lover and partner of over twenty-five years. "Carmen, I don't think I can do this. I completely forgot about Eric having a say in this job. I mean, he could easily tell Mr. Eischer not to hire me and I could lose a chance to showcase my work in Vegas. The MGM Group is only one part of that city. Eischer doesn't call Vegas *his* town just to be cute. He really does own most of it and has stakes in all the rest." Her breath caught in her throat as she tried not to cry. "My past could very well come back to haunt me again."

Carmen crossed the room swiftly and took her into her arms, holding her tightly.

Julia buried her face and hands in the other woman's long blonde hair and let the tears flow.

"Honey, you've come a long way since then. You've faced some pretty horrible stuff from your childhood and made it through. You can do this. It's not about whether or not *they'll* accept that you've changed."

"I know. It's about me accepting that I've changed and accepting myself."

Carmen brushed the tears from Julia's face and kissed her softly. "So, when are you going to accept and *forgive* yourself for your past mistakes?"

Julia sighed deeply as she rested her cheek against Carmen's shoulder. "As soon as I can figure out how to face Jacob one more time and explain myself...maybe then I'll be able to move on."

"Well, let's get your bags packed while you work on that piece of the puzzle. The longer you keep worrying and pacing, the less time you have to figure out what you'll need to take with you to Vegas. I for one don't wish to be up half the night. You have a flight to catch early tomorrow morning and you know what a bear I am without enough sleep."

"What did I ever do to deserve someone like you in my life?"

Carmen smiled and Julia's heart raced. It was the very same smile that hooked her from the first instant she laid eyes on her. "You stole my heart the moment you walked into that play party our friends planned to introduce you and some others into the lifestyle. I couldn't take my eyes off you that night. I knew right from that moment you'd be the best damn sub I would ever have, or want to have. Kitten, don't you know how much I love you?

"Yes, I do." Julia kept her arm around Carmen as she led her down the hallway to their private quarters. "Every single day of my life for the last thirteen years I've thanked Lady Fate for showing me my heart always belonged to you. I denied my feelings for you for so long and yet, you still stood by me even at my worst. I would've died if *She* hadn't intervened."

Carmen hugged her tighter. "The Goddess answered my prayers that too. You were living on the edge back then. I didn't know what else to do but let you go. You needed to find out what and who you really wanted in your life. All I could do was hope you'd choose me."

"I did choose you, Carm and continue to choose you every single day since. You're right, though. I need to see Jacob and get that part of my past behind me once and for all, so I can finally give you the wedding you deserve."

"I don't need a ceremony to prove how much we love each other. I have you by my side now and that's all that matters to me."

"So you've said many times through the years, but I know you. I've seen your eyes light up when our friends talk of their wedding days. I want you to have those stories too. You're my heart, my soul, as well as my Mistress. Let me do this for you, please." Julia wanted so badly to give her lover the one thing she desired most, but would never admit it out loud.

"How about we get you through this trip to Vegas before we start making plans for a wedding?" Carmen brushed Julia's bangs across her forehead and then trailed her cool fingertips down her flushed cheek. "I wish I could be there with you for the whole trip, but I *will* join you as soon as I finish up the last of the hospital board meetings. You can count on it."

"I'm going to hold you to that. Vegas *is* the marriage capital of the world, you know."

Carmen chuckled softly. "You've got your heart set on this, don't you?"

"Yes, Mistress. I would do anything to show the world just how much I love you." Julia knelt before Carmen with her hands behind her back awaiting further instructions."

"Like I said, the best damn sub I could ever wish to have."

Chapter 2

February 12th, Present Day, Las Vegas

Eric Hartley sighed heavily and decided to just give in. Steve was right. The photos of the artwork Julia sent over last week were stunning. He couldn't come up with one logical excuse to not consider her for the job, but his mind never remained logical when it came to Ms. Santos. He still felt as if someone punched him in the gut whenever he heard her name even though it had been thirteen years since he saw her last. Well, it'd been that long since he tossed her out of the intensive care unit where his brother fought for his life—because of her.

"Are you ever going to tell me why you've been so resistant to having Julia do the art for Saints and Sinners?" Steve Eischer wasn't a man to beat around the bush. If he wanted to know something, he'd get the answers sooner rather than later, but in this case Eric needed to back off. It wasn't his story to tell.

"It's water under the bridge now. Let's just say she was a big part of Jake's life thirteen years ago and it's a time of our lives I'd rather not dwell on if you don't mind. Anyway, it's my brother's story to tell and as you keep reminding me, I have to learn to separate my personal life from business decisions if I want to make it in Vegas."

Steve laughed loudly. "Of all the things I've taught you through the last thirteen years, *that's* the one area both of us have trouble with, my friend." He pointed to the photos spread out on the desk. "These are the future of our clubs. Julia could be a great asset and I need to know I can count on you to work with her if I decide to give her the job."

"You can. For me, it's never been a question if she could do the work, but I want to see her in person and how she handles working with your ideas. The Julia I knew wouldn't listen to what her clients wanted. Instead, she'd convince them whatever she did would be good enough and how they should be the ones happy she even agreed to do a piece for them in the first place."

"I didn't get that impression from her. She seems to be genuinely excited about hearing our ideas and promised to come up with a few sketches during our meeting today. Not to change the subject, but I'm not the only one looking forward to her visit. Quinn's brother is really excited Julia's coming to town."

Eric smiled broadly. "Yeah, Derek would love to have her opinion of the pieces he did for the clubs. Hell, he could set up a little museum showcasing his tats alone and it would be a hit. I guess having fresh eyes see his portraits could give him the boost he needs to go ahead with his plans to open a gallery next to the Tattoo Parlor in the Mandalay Bay."

"Julia's a big name in the art world and can give him the critical eye he can't get from family and friends or from the groupies following him around in between his tour dates. I don't know how he handles it all. I get exhausted just thinking about it."

"You're one to talk. Until Quinn walked into your life you burned the candle at both ends and in the middle. For a while there, I was convinced you were a robot, a very rich one, but a robot nonetheless. Speaking of Quinn, when will she and Jake get here, so I can get some one on one time with my niece and nephew?"

Steve chuckled as he put the photos back into the manila envelope they came in. "Darryl called and said the jet landed about 10 minutes ago. With the traffic this time of day, they should be here within the hour, maybe less with Darryl at the wheel. Of course all that hinges on their luggage getting unloaded swiftly. I never realized how much is needed to transport two babies across town, let alone from San Francisco to Vegas."

Eric laughed. "You were the one who insisted on making one of the guest rooms in the penthouse into a nursery. I warned you about the mountains of diapers and bottles a pair of toddlers would need."

"That you did." He glanced at his cell phone as a buzz alerted him to an incoming. "It's from Quinn. The twins are still fast asleep in the back of the limo while Darryl and Jake try to squeeze the luggage into the trunk. They should be leaving the airport sooner than we anticipated."

"And Julia's supposed to arrive in about three hours."

"You can't keep them apart forever you know." Steve slowly smiled. "It's time your big brother confronted Julia once and for all, don't you think?"

Damn! Can't hide anything from Steve. "Yeah, but it doesn't mean I won't have a knot in my stomach the whole time she's here. There's a lot of unfinished business between them and you of all people know how messed up Jake was when he first met Quinn. If it wasn't for your help, he never would have her in his life now, or ever."

"True, but let's not get too worried about all of that now. They'll be here soon enough and while you spend some time with my godchildren, I'll get your brother to tell me the whole story."

* * * *

Chapter 3

Thirteen years ago, Los Angeles

"How many times do we have to keep discussing this, Jacob? I need you here in L.A. *with* me. Not in some ass backwards farming town back east." Julia piled her raven black hair on top of her head in yet another style. Her hazel eyes blazed at Jacob's reflection behind hers in the dressing table mirror. "Your mother will have other birthdays. I'll only have one gallery opening and I need you by my side." A few wisps of hair wouldn't do as Julia commanded, sending her completely over the edge. She slammed her fist against the mirror, shattering it into several pieces. One jagged edged shard embedded itself into her forearm.

Jacob rushed forward and pulled her away from the rest of the glass. "Hold still. Let me take a look at it. Don't you know you're not supposed to just pull—?"

Before he could stop her, Julia wrapped the fingers of her left hand around the sharp bit of mirror and yanked it out of her arm, slashing her wrist with it as she went. Blood rapidly oozed and then suddenly gushed from the wound in spurts. "Jesus Christ, Julia! What the hell are you doing?" Jacob grabbed her robe from the back of the dressing table chair and bound her arm with it. He made her sit on the bed, away from the rest of the broken mirror and pulled his cell phone from his pocket.

Jacob felt grateful his EMT training became second nature for him. Otherwise, he could've been one of those people who panicked in situations like this. He wasn't looking forward to spending another night in the emergency room or trying to explain to the doctors how his girlfriend managed to injure herself once again.

Julia held her injured arm close to her chest then slowly rocked back and forth.

Jacob worried about her having a nervous breakdown. She'd always been a bit over the top, but tonight her behavior went beyond erratic even for her.

She grabbed his arm with her free hand and dug her nails into his flesh. "Baby, please don't leave me! Can't you see I'm a wreck without you? Just the thought of you not being here for my—our grand opening party has my stomach in knots. I can't do it without you. You're my muse. Without you, none of this would be possible. What would people think if you weren't there?" Large tears rolled down her rosy cheeks, with more threatening to fall from her eyes now wild with fright.

Jacob wondered what the hell Julia was afraid of now. Was it really the idea of him leaving or just that he wouldn't be there at her beck and call whenever she wanted? Jacob already heard it all many times before. Each time, he swore he wasn't going to fall for it again, but his heart just wouldn't let him turn his back on her. Not only did he feel afraid Julia would really go over the edge if he did leave her now, he was terrified she just might hurt someone else in the process.

No matter how many times they went through this, he still wanted to do everything in his power to make her smile, even if just for a few hours. If being her escort to her gallery opening would accomplish that, then he simply must do it. No questions about it. He hoped his mother would understand. Julia needed him and God help him, he loved her and needed her too.

Jacob helped her finish dressing and together, they headed down to the lobby of their building. If luck was on his side, the doorman would already have a cab waiting to take them to the hospital, yet again. They'd been there so many times over the last six months alone he wouldn't be surprised if a new hospital wing hadn't been named in her honor by now.

* * * *

Chapter 4

Julia's mind raced, replaying the phone conversation with a woman claiming to be her mother about an hour before Jacob found her at her dressing table. She denied being the one the woman was looking for, but then hung up on her when she hit Julia with a bombshell.

"You look so much like your grandmother did at your age. I have the photo album right here in front of me and that picture of you in the paper is like looking at her twin."

"I'm not sure why you felt the need to tell me that or how you got my number but—"

"She's dead. My mother is dead and I thought her only granddaughter would want to be there for her funeral, but I guess you're too busy with the new life you made for yourself to bother with your family."

"I'm sorry for your loss, but I'm not your daughter. My parents died years ago."

"Yeah, I bet that's what you've told everyone out there in snooty L.A. You wouldn't want all of those rich friends of yours to find out where you really come from, now would you?"

Julia had heard enough and hung up on the woman before she could spew any more evil remarks. Her voice sounded exactly the same as it did when she left. Hearing it again, brought back so many horrible memories of being stuck in that filthy house with a woman who never wanted her in the first place and only found her useful when she became old enough to offer up to her husband. What kind of woman lets her husband fuck her child night after night while ignoring her muffled cries and screams?

It had been her grandmother who saved her. Apparently, the sweet woman stashed a very large amount of money away in a bank account for Julia. The memory remained so vivid, even now all these years later. It'd been the evening before her sweet sixteen birthday party and for some reason, Julia's mother allowed her to stay the night with her grandmother. Big mistake on her part, because it was the last time any of them ever saw the teen. Her grandmother stuffed Julia's purse with cash, a bus ticket to California and a list of people she could stay with until she could take care of herself.

Julia never tapped into the bank account her grandmother set up for her. She'd been afraid someone would trace it and find her. She worked too hard, slinging hash at broken down diners during the day and running the concession stand at the movie theater at night to jeopardize her freedom. Those first few years were tough, but there was no way in hell she'd go back to the nightmare she'd been forced to endure since she was six years old. Most of the time, she didn't know if she was coming or going, but no matter how bad it got for her, she never used one more penny her grandmother set aside for her. She couldn't take the chance someone would be watching the account and come looking for her.

Now, over sixteen years later, someone did. *Fuck!*

Seeing the shard of mirror in her arm made her remember the pain she suffered at the hands of her mother and her stepfather. So many nights she wished for a way out. Now that same woman tried to bring her back into that hell and her mind snapped. *I can't go back to that again, not ever. What would people say if they found out?*

The cab slowed to turn into the parking lot of the hospital. Jacob's arm tightened around her as they came to a stop in front of ER entrance. "Come on, honey. Let's get you inside so they can take care of your arm. You're going to need a few stitches."

What would Jake think of me if he found out? She'd created the best sculptures and paintings of her career—all because Jake was in her life. If he found out about her past, he wouldn't want to stick around and have to deal with all of her emotional baggage. Hell, she could see it in his eyes now. All of her demands on his time, keeping him away from his family, and changing him into one of the most sought after male models were all part of her need to be in complete control. He would end up leaving her, but she didn't want to think about it now. She needed him as her muse and maybe even something more. She knew he loved her, but still she felt the need to make him prove it to her time and time again. "You'll stay with me every step of the way? I mean, they'll probably end up keeping me overnight again. You'll be with me until I fall asleep like the last time?"

"For as long as they let me." He kissed her forehead as they walked through the doors. "Come on, let's get you checked in. It looks like they have a full house tonight."

Julia groaned. "Great. That's all I need right now."

Jacob laughed. "Don't worry. I'm sure they'll be able to wrangle up a private room for you eventually, but you may have a bit of a wait to get it."

"Wanna bet?" Julia settled into the wheel chair and winked at her lover of two years. In her element now, she knew it was time to put on the charm and receive all the perks that came with being one of the local celebrities. "I'll get my own room just like before. When they find out how much stress I've been under getting ready for the gallery opening, they'll understand why I made the silly mistake of pulling that mirror out of my arm the way I did. If it wasn't for your fast thinking, I would've bled to death right there in our bedroom."

Jacob sighed and rubbed the stubble on his chin. "I really don't want to think about what would've happened. It doesn't matter now. I was there and able to help you out this time, but honey, we really have to find you another way to work through the stress."

Julia waved him off. "Yes, baby. I promise you I'll find another outlet to relieve all the stresses in my life."

* * * *

Chapter 5

Just as she predicted, her admittance to the hospital went smoothly and no one batted an eye when she explained to them how she cut her arm. Julia told them the truth and then basked in all the fuss and fanfare showered upon her by the nurses and the others in the waiting room. She loved the attention, but she knew all of it was taking a toll on Jacob.

She didn't put up a fuss nor beg him to stay with her as she'd done many times before. Instead, she pretended to be asleep when he kissed her forehead as he got up to leave. She murmured softly and fluttered her eyes a bit before turning over and snuggling her pillow. She kept her eyes closed and her breathing steady until she knew Jacob walked safely down the hallway. She could guess he stopped one more time to chat with the nurses before going home for the night. Julia wondered if that hot little red headed nurse would be one of her caretakers. What she wouldn't give for a night alone with that little firecracker!

Instead of enjoying the fabulous fantasy for a few moments longer, Julia's guilt got the best of her again. Jacob stood by her through everything even when it meant giving up time with his own family. He repeatedly chose her and her needs over his own. *Why can't I do the same for him? Why do I feel so out of control when I'm with Jake?*

Her entire life in L.A. started with her taking control of her life and not allowing anyone or anything to steal that from her again, but now she found herself torn between wanting to lose control and needing to be *in* control. The battle seemed to be tearing her apart at the moment and only one thing could get her centered again. Julia needed the adrenaline rush zipping through her body whenever a certain doctor did what he'd been told and fucked her silly. She'd give him a few more minutes to show up before she'd start paging him.

She pulled her purse out of the drawer in the nightstand and quickly found her contact case. Tonight, she'd worn the hazel lenses and intended on keeping with the theme. Only one other person beside herself knew her natural eye color now. Jacob asked her about her ever changing iris shades on many occasions, over the last two years. She hadn't told him nor the one she waited for now. This particular person would piss her off if he didn't hold up his end of their arrangement.

The knock on her door brought a smile to her face as she stashed her purse in the drawer once again. *I knew he wouldn't dare disappoint me.*

"Julia, what on earth are we going to do with you?" Dr. Mario Carlos locked the door to the private hospital room and dimmed the lights. "You know how the nurses love to gossip. Eventually, one of them will put two and two together and figure out you've been faking all of these so called accidents."

"Don't kid yourself. I've not faked anything to get here. You know very well I've been preoccupied lately and under a lot of stress. I wouldn't call these things accidents but more like I've been distracted."

"What? Your boy toy-muse not able to alleviate the stress you have?" He snorted dismissively then turned on the charm once again. "You need professional help and I've got what you need right here." Dr. Carlos held up a small green vial of pills and shook them in front of her face.

She raised her eyebrows and licked her lips. "I'm not one of your other patients who come here for drugs."

Mario shrugged. "You had to have a lot of stitches for that gash in your arm. When the local wears off, you'll wish you had these bad boys."

"Fine. If it will get you to shut up about it, I'll take them." Julia snatched them out of his hand and tossed them into the drawer with her purse. "I don't need drugs from you and you know it."

"Call it what you want but sooner or later, you *will* end up the hot topic around the nurses' station. Some may even think you're doing this on purpose to drum up publicity for your gallery." Mario moved slowly across the room and stood inches from her.

His subtle musky cologne filled her nostrils and set her skin on fire. She wanted him. Now. "Who cares what those nosy bitches think." She reached out and rubbed his already hard cock through his scrubs. "I need *this* pounding the hell out of my pussy right now. So stop talking and start fucking." Julia didn't care what anyone else thought and right now, including Jacob. All she could think about was her current lover's glorious cock filling her to the brim... the one outlet she knew would relieve her of the emotional upheaval the call from her mother set into motion.

Ever since being wheeled through the doors of the hospital, only the anticipation of Mario's tongue darting in and out of her ass and pussy mattered. Just the flick of his tongue over his own lips made her shiver with delight and soak her thong.

The very same thong the good doctor tore from her body seconds after lifting her up to sit on top of sink in her bathroom. Her fingers wound through his dark wavy hair as his mouth plundered hers, taking her breath away. She loved the power she held over this man. Any time, any place she wanted, he always obliged. Tonight would be no exception.

Of course he kept her waiting a good half hour after Jacob left before he graced her with his presence.

She wasn't amused by the delay and couldn't care less if some other patients required his attention. It'd been their arrangement that whenever she showed up, he'd drop whatever and whoever and come running.

Now finally, he sheathed his dick with one of those ribbed condoms she demanded he wear whenever they fucked.

Julia still felt a bit miffed at him, but the feeling of his hands on her bare ass temporarily cleared her mind of all her complaints and the shit with her family.

Mario spread her legs wider, lifting her from the sink as he buried his dick in her dripping cunt.

Julia moaned and sighed as he slowly pulled out and plunged back in repeatedly. Even through it felt fantastic to finally have him fucking her, she wanted more. She wanted to be pounded until she was a quivering glob of jelly. Then maybe the images of her childhood would fade from her mind's eye again. He knew what she desired and yet continued the slow pace, pissing her off anew. "Stop teasing me and give me what I want. Now!" Julia pulled his mouth away from hers, but not before she bit down on his lower lip, nearly drawing blood.

"You'll pay for that, bitch."

Chapter 6

"Promise?"

He pulled out of her abruptly and spun her around, leaving her hands momentarily braced against the sink. He kicked her legs apart and bent her over, so that her swollen outer lips glistened at him.

She shimmied and shook her hips, trying to entice him to enter her again.

He grabbed the bottle of hair conditioner and squeezed a large amount over the crack of her ass, slipping his fingers in and out of her, stretching her inner muscles to accommodate him. "I don't make promises, sweetheart. I'm a man of action." He slid the head of his cock into her ass, feeling her tighten around him and then stretch more. The sensation of her squeezing and releasing his entire member as he continued to glide in was almost more than he could take and nearly made him spill his seed. This time he wasn't about to give her the satisfaction of him exploding inside her. Not yet. He had other plans for his demanding lover.

"Oh, now this is what I'm talking about. I love your kind of action, doctor." Julia panted and struggled to move against him, trying to take control of their session as always.

This time, he wasn't going to allow it. He was tired of taking orders from her all the time. Just once, he wanted to be the one to call the shots. Tonight would be the first of many where Julia learned to work for what she wanted from him. He needed to hear *her* beg for a change.

He reached around her and cupped both of her large full breasts in his hands, pinching her nipples roughly as he pulled her up against him. He kept his cock firmly embedded deep inside her ass,

Her anal muscles spasmed out of control and squeezed his dick. Her head fell back against his shoulder as he nibbled along her neck. "Please, Mario."

"Please, what?" He kneaded her breasts and twisted her nipples even harder, eliciting a whimper from her now.

"Please. Fuck. Me. Fuck me until I scream." Her breathing became labored and her body trembled in his arms.

He knew she was close to erupting. He smiled and bit down on her ear lobe, bringing out yet another primal moan from her. His cock throbbed in response to every move and sound she made, especially when she talked dirty. "God, you know I love your filthy mouth."

Mario moved his hands to Julia's hips, feeling her body shake under his fingertips. He dug his nails into her flesh, pulling her back hard against his body, over and over.

She grunted with each thrust inside of her, dancing on the tips of her toes while keeping her ass in the position he wanted her in. Her cum coated her inner thighs and continued to spurt out of her.

He pounded her harder, thinking about burying his face between her legs and lapping up every last drop of her sweet juices.

She grabbed one of the wash clothes sitting on the sink and shoved it into her mouth barely stifling her screams of ecstasy.

Finally, the always demanding diva became putty in his hands. He smiled at his reflection in the bathroom mirror and continued to pump into her ass. Julia stifled one more scream just as he emptied his own hot cum deep inside her, filling the condom to near bursting. At last, he controlled her and he liked it.

Moments like this with her drove his fantasies nearly every waking moment. There was no way in hell Jacob Hartley gave her what he did. Why else would she arrange so many accidents to wind up back in his ER and in his care? Mario decided now would be the time to make his move and give her an ultimatum. She needed to dump Hartley and go public with their relationship, or it was over.

No woman ever turned him down before and meant it. He could always wear them down to the point where they begged him to fuck them senseless. If he saw a piece of ass he wanted, he got it, including just about every woman he'd worked with at the hospital. Why should this one be any different?

* * * *

Julia stepped out of the shower and into the large fluffy robe Mario held out for her. "Don't worry. I was careful to keep my stitches covered as you directed."

"It would've been much easier if you let me help you. It's the least I can do since you went to such extremes to be with me tonight."

She pulled away from him and out of the steamy bathroom. "You're full of shit. How dare you make assumptions about how I injured my arm? I told all of you the truth. Jacob backed up my story, so you have no *right* to question it."

"Cut the drama, Julia. It's me you're talking to. I know you better than anyone—"

"You haven't got a clue about me or what's going on in my life right now, so don't think for one minute my accident was a ploy to see you. If you weren't on duty, I'd find another to give me what I wanted. You've known that right from the start."

"I didn't sign up to be your boy toy. You've got Hartley for that."

She laughed. "You're exactly what I say you are, Mario. That's what we agreed on when we first met. I gave you explicit ground rules and you agreed. You can't change the rules now. That's not how it works with me."

"Why not? Things change between two people all the time. Circumstances, feelings, and life goals can all change. Why can't we change with it?"

"Because I don't *want* anything to change between us. This is all I need you for. You're the one who's delusional if you think otherwise."

He shook his head and headed for the door. "We'll talk more about this another time. For now, you need your rest and I have several other patients to attend to tonight."

"Please say hello to that yummy ginger Nurse Kathy for me. You really should make an honest woman out of her. Any fool can tell she's madly in love with you."

He spun around and glared at her. "She's got nothing to do with what's going on between you and me. Leave her out of this."

"Aw, is she another one you've been banging in secret? How many does that make now, Doctor? Five? Eight? Ten?" Julia laughed as he stormed out of her room. *I guess it's okay for him to have his toys but he can't be one himself.*

Chapter 7

Thirteen Years Ago,
Realm between Heaven and Earth

The entire far wall of the mountainside chalet was covered with high definition television screens. Modern technology fascinated The Three. They were able to keep track of their human creations, using the very gadgets invented by them.

Lucius in particular, seemed fond of the wireless technology used in cell phones and personal computers. With a few swift clicks on the keyboard of his laptop, all the screens came to life with pictures of the people they were gathered to discuss.

Yeshua, the eldest of the Eternal Siblings, sat in a large, overstuffed easy chair, taking in all the lives playing out on the screens before him. His deep blue eyes scanned through everything in seconds, immediately recognizing those in view.

These humans were the favorites of his sister, Fate. Once again, she wished to plead the case of another of the group. Apparently, this particular human seemed to be special—to Lucius as well.

"Why should we intervene with Julia's life path now?" Yeshua asked. "Isn't enough we're allowing the Guardians to help Quinn and Jacob find each other?

Wouldn't it be wise to just see how it all plays out for the rest from this point on?"

The tall, dark, brooding God of Trials and Tribulations rolled his amber eyes. "As you've pointed out on numerous occasions dear Brother, our interference with any life path affects more than just one creation. By giving Jacob and Quinn their chance to bond on the Island, we've opened up too many other variables for the others. In order to keep them all on their chosen paths, we have to give a nudge here and there." Lucius smiled at Fate. "Your new Guardians should be able to handle all of them, although I think they'll need your help a bit with Julia."

Fate nodded. "Aye. She's been through so much in her life already. She's allowed very few people into her heart and she continues to make poor choices in order to keep her past a secret."

Yeshua stared at the raven haired beauty now occupying all of the screens. "I agree. She's been through enough. No offense, Lucius but I feel you've done your job all too well with her."

"Agreed. I'll not throw more at her, but I can't stop what's already set into motion because of her choices. Her actions are what bring Jacob to the Island in the first place. Once he's there with Quinn, Fate and the Guardians can step in and give her the chance to choose her one true love. From that point on, it's all up to her."

The Goddess Fate smiled and held her hands out to either brother. "Thank you both for allowing me to do this." She squeezed both of their hands tightly, momentarily overcome with emotion. Her emerald green eyes shimmered with tears a moment before they cleared. "She's going to go through a lot of pain before this is over."

The Creator nodded. "That she will, but she'll have her soul mate there with her through it all. She just has to open her eyes and see the heart that's always been bound to her own. Her redemption will ultimately come at a price she has to be willing to pay. Reliving the nightmares of her childhood will be a difficult task for her."

Lucius raised one dark eyebrow. "Here, I thought our sister was the hopeless romantic."

Yeshua chuckled. "I do enjoy a good love story now and again. I believe in giving second chances to all our creations. Between all of these couples we've been discussing today, there are some who've waited far too long to be together." Fate rolled her eyes and smiled.

Yeshua grinned at the sight of his sister picking up another of their younger brother's mannerisms. The two were so much alike and yet neither would ever admit it. He turned his attention back to the discussion at hand. "And no...you don't need to keep reminding me it was my decision to give humans free will in the first place."

Fate turned to tease him a bit. "As the Guardians Daniel and Michael are fond of saying 'that pesky Free Will always gets in the way!' Let's see how Julia's story plays out now, shall we?"

* * * *

Chapter 8

Julia was definitely in her element. All the movers and shakers of the West Coast art world were there for the opening of her gallery—as they should be. She'd been planning the event for nearly two years, right from the moment she first laid her eyes on Jacob at Club 740 in downtown Los Angeles. He was the hottest thing she'd seen in a long time. Well, the hottest man who wasn't already panting and drooling over her that night.

What attracted her to him the most was the fact he actually had the nerve to turn down her invitation to join her at her private table. Apparently he'd arrived with his brother along with a group of friends and had been otherwise occupied. At least that had been the excuse the waitress gave her when she returned the bottle of champagne Julia had sent to his table.

It hadn't stopped her. Determined to have Jacob Hartley and by the end of the night, she had managed to find out from the bartender who he was and where he stayed while in town, celebrating his brother's graduation from UCLA. Letting the goon fuck her against the bar after closing had seemed like a small price to pay. What she didn't expect was having the bouncer take her up the ass at the same time, but what the hell? Not only had she received the information she wanted about Jacob, she'd been guaranteed free booze and admission to the club whenever she walked through the doors.

Being dressed to the nines at the bar hadn't seemed to impress Jacob much, so she had taken another approach. She'd showed up at his hotel room in nothing but a black trench coat and four inch high red stilettos. She offered him three grand a week to model for her exclusively. He'd hesitated only a moment before agreeing to her terms. As soon as he'd signed the contract, she dropped the trench coat she wore and gave him his signing bonus. The things they did to each other that night still made her wet thinking about them, and tonight would be no exception.

Jacob was definitely the hottest male in the gallery and she wanted him. No, waiting for the party to be over wasn't an option. She needed to have him, now. She crossed the room and just barely touched his arm with her fingertips.

He excused himself from the group he'd been talking with and followed her to their private office in the back of the gallery.

As soon as he secured the door behind him, she pinned him against it. "Do you have any idea how much I want to fuck you? If this tux hadn't cost me a bundle, I would have it in shreds right now."

Jacob's smile lit up his face and her thong would have been soaked if she'd been wearing one. "What about all of your friends and perspective buyers? Don't you think they'll miss the guest of honor?"

Julia nipped his lower lip a bit as she slid his jacket off and tossed it on the overstuffed love seat. "Right now, if the staff is doing what I paid them to do, the guests are busy eating, drinking, and talking about my sculptures and paintings."

She removed her dress and dropped it where his jacket lay. "Forget about them for now. I'm so wound up and you have what I need to get me back on track. She pulled him toward her glass topped desk. In one swift motion, she tossed the few papers left there, to the floor. Wearing only her high heels while exposing her Brazilian waxed body, she leaned back and spread her legs wide. Her fingers immediately plunged into her folds to find her clit. As soon as she touched it, she moaned and gushed again.

Within seconds, his mouth replaced her fingers, sucking hard on her already throbbing clit. His fingers worked her cunt toward another round of spasms. Her ass bounced with each thrust of his hand. Jacob's tongue swirled around her clit a few more times before he abruptly pulled away.

"Don't stop, baby. I'm nearly there, again," she panted.

He dropped his pants to the floor, showing her she wasn't the only one going commando.

She smiled and beckoned with her fingers. "Don't keep me waiting, lover. Your dick looks like it could use a woman's touch."

Jacob stroked his cock a few times and licked his lips. "Do you have anyone in mind?"

Julia dipped her fingers into her folds once again and then sucked them clean. "Care to take a wild guess? She held his gaze as she lay back on the desk, brought her knees up toward her chest, and gave him a full shot of her dripping pussy. "This is all the woman you'll ever need."

He grabbed her hips and pulled her back toward the edge of the desk, filling her cunt with his cock. Resting her legs on his chest, and wrapping his arms around her thighs he pumped into her hard and fast.

Just the way she liked it—the way she wanted it from all of her lovers, even the ones she'd tossed aside. Jacob was the only man she'd ever let fuck her without protection. He'd resisted at first, but soon gave in to her wishes. The feeling of riding him bare back was unbelievable to her. She came multiple times with him from that point on and loved every minute of it.

Two years was the longest time a relationship lasted for her with a man. The time had come to end another one. Things were getting a bit complicated with the good Dr. Carlos and she didn't think she could keep it secret for much longer, but no matter. Tonight was her night to shine and she needed her muse by her side to complete the package. "Yes, baby, like that. Fuck me harder. Fill me up. Now!"

Her muse always followed orders during sex. With two more thrusts, Jacob erupted deep inside of her, just as she commanded.

She stroked his stubbly chin and purred. She felt completely relaxed and ready to face the rest of her guests without any more tension. Nothing would ruin her night now. Not even a confrontation with Mario, which she'd been avoiding ever since he arrived and seemed hell bent on getting her alone.

"We better get you back into your sexy dress and me into that tux you paid so much money for, before your friends start searching for us."

She laughed. "We wouldn't want that now would we?"

He helped her off the desk and frowned. "I'm not so sure that wasn't your intention all along, Julia. Did you really think I wouldn't notice you reached behind me to unlock the door before we moved to the desk?"

She smiled and shrugged her shoulders.

"I'm beginning to think you wouldn't mind it if we went at it in the center of the gallery in front of everyone, like a living embodiment of one of your sculptures. What's going on with you? You've been quite the exhibitionist lately."

She closed her eyes and sighed deeply. "Why are you bringing this up again? I thought we settled this when I came home from the hospital. I'm not going to see a shrink and that's that. The only therapy I need is right here, in your arms and in our bed. End of story." Julia slipped into her backless micro-mini dress and headed for the door. "Try not to take too long to rejoin the party. The same people who'll be looking for me...are keeping their eyes on you as well. After tonight, don't be surprised if a career in modeling isn't in your future." She winked and blew him a kiss.

Jacob simply stood there, naked in the middle of their office. He watched her leave while shaking his head.

She closed the door behind her and smoothed her dress over her hips. She made her way back to her

guests and hopefully the biggest sales in her career.
What the hell just happened here? The night has been going on without a hitch. All I wanted was to release some of the built up tension. Can I help it that I need the adrenaline rush from the possibility we could be caught at any time? I thought Jake of all people understood that about me. Why did he have to ruin my night by bringing up the shrink again?

* * * *

Chapter 9

February 12th Present Day, Las Vegas

Julia smiled as she made her way through a sea of travelers, toward the group of limo drivers holding signs. Steve had offered to send one of his jets to bring her to Vegas, but she'd politely declined. She didn't feel right about letting him go through all the expense to bring her to his town, at least not yet. If she got the job, then she'd let him fly her wherever the hell he wanted her to go.

She quickly glanced through all the people holding up signs for the passengers filing through the baggage claim area until she spotted her name. Seeing the regal driver standing there waiting for her made the butterflies in her stomach calm just a bit. She took it as a good sign Mister Vegas Tycoon still wanted her for the job. "I'm Julia Santos."

The driver bowed slightly and flashed a warm smile. "Welcome to Las Vegas, Ms. Santos. I'm Darryl. Mr. Eischer sent me to make sure we get you and your things to the MGM as soon as possible. If you'd point out your luggage, I'll gather everything and we'll be on our way."

"This day keeps getting better and better. I get to be escorted to the hotel by a very handsome man, and I see my two pieces of luggage making their way around the conveyor belt now. I think you're my lucky charm,

Darryl." Julia's phone buzzed against her hip indicating an incoming text. *Quinn and I will meet you for dinner tonight. We'll make the reservations and send you the details. ~Jake.* "Holy shit."

Darryl grabbed the red leather suitcases with ease and turned toward her with a concerned look. "Is everything okay, Ms. Santos? You look like you've seen a ghost."

"You could say that. It's a message from another couple I had hoped would agree to meet with me on this trip. I just got word they said yes. To be honest, I'm more nervous about meeting them than Mr. Eischer."

"Don't you worry one bit. You'll like Quinn right away."

Julia's jaw nearly hit the floor. "How did you know that was who I was talking about?"

"I've been Mr. Eischer's driver for many years. There isn't much I don't know. Besides, Quinn and Jake arrived a few hours before you and I was their driver too. She gave me the heads up to be sure you get to the MGM in style."

"Really? Well, I have to say you're doing a great job so far. If I had to do this myself, I probably would've just turned right around and got on the next flight back home." Julia took a deep breath and held it for a moment before letting it out in a rush. "Can I ask you something?"

"Sure. Might as well spill it. If it's something I can answer, I will." Darryl wheeled the luggage expertly through the sliding glass doors out to where the limo was parked. He loaded up the trunk with her things.

Julia stood next to him and continued to fidget. "Does Jake seem happy with Quinn? I mean truly happy and not just going through the motions."

Darryl studied her for a moment then nodded. "Yes Ma'am. The Hartleys happen to be the happiest couple I know—especially now, with the twins keeping them on their toes. And no, he's not just going through the motions. It took a hell of a lot to get those two together. They are, as they say—soul mates." He held the car door open for her.

Julia slid into the limo while her eyes filled with tears. "Once again, you've made my whole day. That's exactly what I wanted to hear. Thirteen years ago, I thought I destroyed any hope of Jacob ever finding his happily ever after. It's good to hear he's made it through the all the pain I caused him."

Darryl reached for her hand and squeezed gently. "Ms. Santos, you wait and see for yourself tonight. Those two have made it through hell fire to be together. It's time you let go of the guilt you're feeling over the past. Las Vegas is a great place to do that. How about I scoot you on over to the MGM and get you settled before you begin another chapter in your own life?"

"If I didn't know better, I'd say you were one of the guardian angels sent to watch over those of us who've lost our way."

He winked. "Who says I'm not?" He closed the door and moved to the front of the car before Julia could answer.

Well, it wouldn't be the first time I met one, that's for sure. The limo pulled out into the traffic leaving the airport and Julia let her mind wander back to the time when it all began to unravel for her and Jacob. All of it was her fault. If she would've just been honest with him from the start, instead of holding on to him far longer than she should have, who knows what would have happened in between then and now. "Why did I ever let him fall in love with me?"

The memories flooded through her, bringing the pain back into her heart as sharp as the day she lived through it the first time. She'd used sex as both a comfort and a manipulation to get what she thought she wanted. Back then, she didn't think she needed help to get through anything. She'd just bury it all and go on. Unfortunately for Julia and the few she let into her life then, it was the wrong decision, one which nearly cost Jacob his life.

* * * *

Chapter 10

Thirteen years ago, Los Angeles

She watched Jacob greet several of their guests. He looked happy and relaxed, making those around him feel the same. Julia loved to watch him tell the stories of how the artwork was made. His deep blue eyes twinkled with delight as he shared a few of the naughty details.

The women next to him blushed and the men smiled knowingly.

She didn't have to worry about him fitting in with her friends any longer. Even if he might be uncomfortable, he no longer let it show. This development freed Julia up to work the room herself without having to worry about him hiding out in a corner, like he used to do early on in their relationship.

All the good feelings were dashed the moment her eyes settled on Mario Carlos making his way toward her. *Fuck!* Julia hoped to be able to avoid the doctor for a bit and thought her gallery opening would be a safe zone, since she didn't send him an invitation. She knew for damn sure he wasn't on the approved list at the door either. She'd have a few choice words with her assistant, Darla about it later.

This was the sort of shit she paid the woman top money to handle. No wonder Julia's stress level went through the roof all the time. It didn't help matters when she herself had to follow up on every single detail she expected her assistant to handle for her. More often than not over the last few weeks, Darla had been dropping the ball. Julia made a mental note to talk to the girl about these screw ups. She needed to either get her act together, or find another job. Period.

Tonight of all nights, she found herself smack dab in the middle of a situation she didn't want to be in. What pissed her off more than anything? Mario knew the gallery was the most important thing in her life, and yet there he was, right at her side trying to steer her away from her guests into a private corner. After pulling away from him at least a half dozen times, she came to her breaking point. Feeling his hand on her bare back sent her over the edge. Hissing through clenched teeth, so no one else could hear, Julia made her irritation known. "Move away from me, or I'll have security escort you out."

"Really? You'd cause a scene here in front of everyone?" He smiled and moved his arm around her waist.

Julia stepped away again, and greeted a few more guests then turned her attention back to him. "I wouldn't be the one causing the scene. You're an uninvited guest and I have every right to have you kicked out of here. So far, you've had the good sense not to introduce yourself as my personal physician and that's probably why I've let you stay this long. Back off now, before Jake catches you harassing me." She slid away from him to join another group of guests interested in a few of her pieces.

Unfortunately, Mario followed her and once again placed his hand in the middle of her back.

This time, she searched the crowd for Jacob and smiled. “Shit’s about to hit the fan. You’ve pushed me and Jake too far this time.”

“Bring it, bitch. I’m not afraid of your boy toy.”

* * * *

Jacob leaned against the bar and watched Julia work the room. She definitely loved being the center of attention at all times. Once again he wondered if there was anything she wouldn’t do to make sure she remained the talk of the town. Her sculptures were beyond what most would call sensual. Some had actually labeled them borderline pornographic. Anyone off the street would be able to tell she used herself as one of the models. The details she included, right down to the dagger tattoo on her right hip, left nothing to the imagination.

Her attention to detail included the characteristics of her male model—Jacob himself. His shoulder length hair, tattoos, scars and even his fully erect cock were all present and accounted for in various sculptures as well as a few of her paintings. She hadn’t been kidding when she called him her muse. Until she’d met him, it’d been nearly a year since she created anything new.

Now here they were, two years later with a gallery full of her work and packed with the other artists, collectors, and critics in the art world of Los Angeles. There were even a few who'd flown in from New York. Every one of their guests wanted a moment of her time, and one in particular caught Jacob's attention.

Dr. Mario Carlos seemed to nonchalantly slip in next to Julia while she held court with a couple who were interested in the bronze sculpture of two lovers entwined.

Jacob kept his eyes on the doctor as more people joined Julia's little discussion group.

The man appeared to move closer and closer to her, until he neatly slipped his arm behind her and rested his hand at the middle of her back.

The appearance of intimacy between the two caused the hair on the back of Jacob's arms to stand on end and made his mouth go dry. *What the hell?* He grabbed another shot of whiskey from the line of them set up on the bar, and tossed it back without looking away from Julia and her group.

He watched as she continually scanned the crowd until her eyes locked with his. Her smile told him she struggled to keep cordial and needed him right away.

Julia edged away from Dr. Carlos and focused her attention on yet another perspective buyer, while leaving Darla to handle the delivery details with the first couple.

From Jacob's vantage point, Julia's dismissive behavior didn't appear to go over too well with the doctor, who gulped down his drink and signaled to the servers for another as he attempted to slip in close to her again.

Jacob had seen enough.

It wasn't the first time another man hit on Julia, and it wouldn't be the last. However, something about Mario Carlos rubbed him the wrong way, especially his behavior with Julia in front of the other guests. He seemed to be crossing multiple boundaries.

Jacob didn't like it at all. One thing for certain, he wasn't about to let the man continue to work his charms on her, not tonight—not ever.

He strode through the room as rapidly as he could, weaving in and out of the various clusters of guests, never taking his eyes off of her.

Another smile slowly formed on her full ruby red lips.

His cock stirred. He fought the urge to pull her into his arms and kiss her right there in front of everyone, especially Dr. Carlos. Why should he stoop to their level of mind games? He knew Julia loved him in her own way. He didn't need any huge public displays of affection to prove it. It would be his bed she'd be in later tonight.

When he approached, Julia wrapped her arms around him, holding him close. "There you are Jacob, darling! I was just telling everyone all the fun we had creating the poses for the sculptures. Mario didn't believe we actually did those things depicted in the artwork. He thinks it's all make-believe, a fantasy if you will."

Jacob smiled and took a glass of champagne from the server who suddenly appeared on his right. "Whether he believes it or not doesn't matter. We know what went into making those sculptures and paintings.

Many hours. One on one." He raised his glass and the others in the group followed, except the now red-faced doctor. "Here's to Julia, for making *my* fantasies come to life every single day. May her art inspire you to fulfill a few spicy ones of your own.

Julia kissed him softly then raised her glass. "Here's to the man who's inspired it all. He's more than fulfilled *my* fantasies. Please join me and raise your glasses in honor of my muse and the star of every woman's erotic dreams, Jacob Hartley!"

Cheers erupted throughout the gallery. This felt like the happiest night of his life. So, why did he feel like this was the beginning of the end of their relationship?

* * * *

Chapter 11

February 12th, Present Day, Las Vegas

Standing outside of Saints and Sinners, Julia stared at the larger than life portrait of a beautiful fallen angel. The eyes drew her right in and held her there, momentarily speechless. The model, while beyond stunning, was a hot mess of curves to die for. She sported a short, messy, pixie cut hairstyle and eyes the color of the ocean. "Damn. Those come fuck me eyes really do exist."

"Yes they do, and you'll be meeting the woman behind those eyes tonight."

Julia spun around and came face to face with another flash from her past. Eric might even be better looking than she remembered. In fact, she'd go as far as to say he'd gotten hotter with age. "Eric Hartley, I never thought we'd be meeting like this after all these years."

To her surprise, he offered her his hand.

"Neither did I, but here we are." He shook her hand with genuine warmth. "Steve is excited to get your input on the ideas he has for the club and if he likes what you come up with, he'll want you to help with the remodels of the others as well."

"Wow. I knew he was interested in my work, but shouldn't he check out a few more sketches before he makes a decision?" Julia felt flattered but scared shitless at the same time. The doubts kept creeping up and making her nauseous. It must've shown in her expression too.

"Relax, Julia. He loves what he's seen so far. Just show him what you can do. There's no question about your talent, but to be totally honest with you, I wasn't too keen on hiring you for this job. I only know the Julia from thirteen years ago."

"Understood. What changed your mind?"

"Honestly, it was remembering everything Jake and Quinn went through to find each other. For a while there, I thought they'd never get down the aisle. They had to overcome a lot of obstacles to get to where they are today. Everyone deserves a second chance—even you." He reached over and squeezed her arm gently. "And the sketches you sent over last week were exactly what we've been talking about for the remodels."

Julia smiled and nodded. "Thank you for giving me the opportunity to show you what I can do, but I have to ask. The place is already filled with amazing artwork. Why would you want to change it? Who did this portrait? It's breathtaking." She looked at it one more time and snapped her head back toward Eric. "Wait, you said I'd meet the woman behind the eyes tonight. Is that Quinn?"

Eric laughter filled her ears. "Hang on there, woman. Give me a chance to answer the first question before you start firing off more. Steve and his partners like to keep all the clubs fresh and new, but they don't want to completely change everything. We want to get some new pieces in here to enhance what we have going already. The portrait is one thing that won't be changing at all. It's the key piece here in the entryway to the club and the casino patrons love it. The artist is Derek Quartermarsh, the adopted brother of the model, Quinn Quartermarsh Hartley."

"I've heard of Derek. Doesn't he have a tattoo parlor here in Vegas too?"

"Yes, he does. It's over at the Mandalay Bay. Make sure you stop by while you're in town. He has books filled with his work. He's just returned from three month tour with his band, Quarter to Three."

"My partner, Carmen got to see them when she was in Orlando for a medical conference and she was hoping he'd be back in Vegas now. It would be fun to have him design a couple tats for us while we talk about his art and maybe catch him on stage at the House of Blues."

Eric nodded. "Derek made it a point for me to ask that you stop in, so I'm sure he'd be thrilled to use you and your partner as his canvas. As for his schedule with the band, I believe they'll be playing there this weekend."

"If his tats are anything like his paintings, I'd be honored to sit in his chair." Julia continued to stare at the portrait, appreciating the detail Derek put into capturing his sister's essence on canvas. "Quinn has that classic beauty all artists kill to find in a model. No wonder Jake fell in love with her. Hell, I'm falling just looking at her image."

"It was her smile that grabbed me the first day we met." Steve Eischer joined them while Julia was engrossed in the portrait.

She nearly jumped out of her skin when she heard his deep baritone next to her ear.

"Ms. Santos, I hope I didn't keep you waiting too long out here. I was on a conference call with a few of my partners. They're as anxious to know if you've accepted the position as I am."

Julia shook the hand of one of the richest men in the country, if not the world, and prayed she wouldn't pass out right there on the spot. "Please, call me Julia. Thank you both for asking me to come out to show you my ideas."

"I'll call you Julia, if you agree to call me Steve and let me take you inside the club. You're looking a bit pale. Did you eat anything before your flight?"

"Now that you mentioned it, I've been so nervous about our meeting, I haven't eaten since lunch—yesterday."

Steve's emerald eyes twinkled. "I thought as much. Come on inside. Let's get some food into you while I tell you a bit more about what I envision for Saints and Sinners and her sister clubs."

Julia immediately felt at ease. "I hope you don't mind if I sketch while you share your ideas. It helps me to brainstorm with my clients."

Eric smiled as he opened the club doors for them. "Now that's *not* the Julia I remember. This meeting has already turned out better than I'd anticipated."

Julia felt her eyes sting with the start of tears. If she could impress Eric with how much she's changed over the years, perhaps there was hope she could get through to Jacob and get him to forgive her. "Thank you for saying that. It means more to me, than you'll ever know."

Steve pulled out her chair at one of the private tables just off the dance floor. "A little birdy told me about your dinner with Quinn and Jake tonight. If it makes you feel any better, he's a bundle of nerves too."

"Really? I don't want to intrude on their lives. I'm at a place in mine where I need to make amends to the people I hurt in the past. I've gone through years of therapy to get to this point. It's time I face him and own up to my part in the accident that nearly killed him."

"He held on to the baggage for many years. Until he met Quinn, I didn't think he'd ever settle down or let himself fall in love with anyone. He's moved on to a better place now and it's because of Quinn that he's agreed to meet with you tonight. I know my brother. He would rather just let the past stay there and move on, but it was the letter from your partner Carmen that convinced both of them to see you." Eric dug right into his sandwich with gusto.

Julia giggled.

"What?"

"I see your appetite hasn't changed one bit."

Both men laughed.

Julia felt confident for the first time in weeks. "Now, how about you tell me a bit more about your vision for this place? I'm thinking we keep the basic theme with the angels and fallen angels but add a bit more spice with sculptures that complement Derek's fabulous paintings."

"Darlin' you've read my mind."

Chapter 12

December20th, Thirteen Years Ago, Los Angeles

"As much as I would love to spend the next few weeks with you and your family Jake, I just can't get away. The gallery is taking up all my time right now, and I've picked up several more commissions since the opening. I have to get three of those pieces done in time for delivery on the first."

"I understand all that but my mother made a special trip out here to meet you and spend the holidays with my sister's family. This is our first Christmas without Pop. We agreed not to spend anymore holidays without all of us under one roof to celebrate. This is the perfect opportunity for you to meet them. Besides, the gallery can run without you for a few days."

He just didn't understand how scared she really was to meet his family face to face, especially his mother, Katrina. Julia knew without a doubt, the woman would see right through her, the moment she laid eyes on her. She didn't want to be judged by anyone right now. Too much was at stake to take that risk. She needed Jacob to keep her creativity flowing for just a little while longer. After that, she wasn't sure where their relationship would go. He'd been the only one of her male lovers who convinced her to relinquish a bit of the control she needed to have in her life.

With him, she could be vulnerable and not be afraid he would toss her away immediately, after getting what he wanted from her. Unfortunately, her old demons continued to rear their ugly heads, and the security Jacob provided didn't carry over during the times they were apart. That's why she held onto him so tightly. Without him as her safety net, Julia was sure her creativity would dry up and everything she worked so hard for with her art would disappear, never to return again. Without her art, she would be nothing.

Only one other person ever treated her with the same respect and dignity as Jacob. Her best friend and confidant, Carmen...exactly who she needed now to make heads or tails out of the mess she'd made with keeping Mario around. Carmen had warned her, he would try to get more from her than she was willing to give, but Julia didn't listen. She just couldn't resist the rush she felt while bringing Mario and men like him, to their knees. Unfortunately, the more she dipped into that candy jar, the more she craved and the emptier she felt. Funny, the only times in her life she ever felt fulfilled were those she spent with Jacob or Carmen.

"Babe? Where'd you go? You looked a million miles away. "

Julia shook her head. "I'm sorry, honey. I have so much going on in my head and I must've have zoned out for a second there." She took a deep breath and let it out slowly before she spoke again. The last thing she wanted was to fight with him, but she needed to try to make him understand her side a bit more. "I've had to sacrifice many holidays over the years to get this far. I don't want anything to jeopardize the gallery's success. I thought you understood that and we were on the same page." She continued to pack her overnight bag to get ready for her road trip. This time though, she planned to start with a long overdue visit with Carmen. Julia was sure her friend would be able to help her focus and get back on track.

Being under Carmen's care always helped her sort through the chaos in her life. *Why the hell have I stayed away from her for so long? I wouldn't blame her if she tossed me aside after putting our friendship on the back burner. Hell, who am I kidding? It was becoming much more than a friendship for both of us. Maybe that's why I pulled back and took up with so many different lovers, tossing them aside when I got what I needed from them? All except for Jake. He's so much like Carmen, it scares me.*

He stood behind her and wrapped his arms around her waist. "I know better than anyone how much you've put into the gallery. I just feel you need to give yourself a break from all the stress for a few days. Please. It would mean the world to me if we spent Christmas with my family." He nibbled on her ear lobe

His nibbling elicited a moan from her. Julia smiled. She knew Jacob would pull out all the stops to convince her to spend the holidays with him. She even recognized it as one of her own little tricks to get him to go with what she wanted. "Oh that's so not fair. You know my ears are a hot zone for me."

"Uh huh." He trailed kisses down her neck as she leaned back against his chest. His hands cupped her breasts through her form fitting tank top, pinching her already rock hard nipples. "I want my family to get to know the woman I love, the one I want to spend the rest of my life with."

She turned in his arms to face him. "It's not that easy. Your brother can't stand me. He's said as much to my face the day you moved in with me here and didn't follow him to Vegas. I'm sure he's filled your mother's head with all sorts of lies. I've only talked to your sister over the phone. I think she resents the fact you're here with me and not down there, helping her and her husband with their business. I mean, really? Can you see yourself running a group of doggie day care facilities now that you've enjoyed a taste of the good life here in L.A.?"

"Just because their business has nothing to do with your circle of artist friends doesn't mean it's a waste of time."

Her head throbbed. She wasn't explaining herself the way she wanted and knew she was making things worse. "That's not what I meant and you know it. I just see better things for you in your future as a model. I don't want to argue with you about this stuff anymore." She rested her forehead against his shoulder as he held her tight. "Are you sure it's what you want? Spending the rest of your life with me could end up bringing you a lot of heartache. What if—?"

He cradled her face with both hands and kissed her. "What if nothing. I love you with all of my heart. I can't see myself with anyone else but you."

Tears filled her eyes. "No man has ever said that to me before and meant it, Jake. You have no idea how much it means to me."

"I do. I have right from the start. I wouldn't push you this hard about meeting my family now if it didn't mean so much to me. I need you by my side this year in order to make it through."

Her heart nearly broke in two. She remembered how much he suffered when he lost his father the year before. She'd begged off going to the funeral with him, citing commitments she just couldn't break. It was time she finally came clean about some of it. "You know I still feel horrible for not being with you for your father's funeral, but I didn't want to intrude on your family's grief." Plus, she hadn't wanted to face the accusing eyes from Eric, blaming her for taking Jacob away from them while the patriarch of their family was dying. "I didn't realize how much this all meant to you because I've been so wrapped up in my own world. I'm sorry. I'll have Darla clear my schedule for next week. My clients will just have to understand. You've been by my side through all of this, and now it's my turn. My place is with you."

His lips covered hers as their tongues twirled and sparred with each other in the battle for control.

She loved the way he kissed her, allowing her a few moments of dominance before stealing it back again, leaving her breathless with need. He pulled her tank top over her head and tossed it to the floor while she quickly undid his belt and zipper of his pants. Sliding her hands inside, she caressed his growing erection with just her fingertips—enough to elicit a feral growl from her lover as he picked her up and carried her to their king sized bed.

She slipped out of her boy shorts and slid up along the down comforter to lie on the pillows, reaching for him as he got rid of the rest of his clothes to join her. “Show me how much you love me, baby. Make me feel it. Make me believe it.”

His eyes grew dark as he held her gaze, accepting the challenge.

For a moment, she thought he might tell her to go to hell for doubting how he felt about her, but it wasn’t his style. He would show her what she craved to be shown, but she sensed something changed within him. Gone was the eagerness to please her, and in its place a desire so white hot, it consumed her right on the spot. No longer did she feel the need to dominate him every minute they spent together. Instead, she gave herself to him willingly, enjoying every moment.

He slowly worked his way down her body, licking, nibbling and tasting as he went.

She cooed and sighed every step of the way, her body no longer under her control, but his.

His touch set her skin on fire, while his mouth fanned the flames to a raging inferno.

Nothing and no one else mattered to her but the two of them right here and now. Jacob’s lips sealed over her clit, drawing out a deep guttural moan from her. No man could eat her out like him, and tonight he seemed to be in rare form, a man on a mission. His silky tongue glided in and out of her folds with deliberate slow motions.

Her body became overcome with need to have him and yet he took her even higher.

While he sucked her throbbing clit, his fingers filled up her pussy and stretched her anus.

"Oh, my god, that feels fucking fantastic. Don't stop." She was nearly breathless from the orgasm building inside her but she wanted more, so much more.

He teased and feathered her hot, wet folds until the comforter beneath them became drenched with her juices. He slid back up along her body, slowly snaking his tongue along a burning trail to her tits.

Her nipples were so erect they hurt, just the way she liked them. The slightest touch, even a whisper of his hot breath over them sent her over the edge, her cunt twitching with the need to be completely filled with his cock. Unable to keep still any longer, she pulled her legs up and wrapped them around his hips. "Fuck me now, Jake. Let me have that glorious dick of yours deep inside me."

Her breathing quickened as the head of his cock eased into her—much too slow for her needs. She tried to pull him inside her.

He blocked her at every turn. Jacob only smiled at her attempts and held his position until she finally relaxed enough for him to tug her arms over her head. He quickly bound them to the leather straps attached to the headboard.

She returned his Cheshire cat grin as she settled into the restraints. She loved the feel of the strap around her wrist and in her palm. Having her hands bound while she was willingly ravaged by a man had always been a fantasy of hers, and now she could mark it off her bucket list. “When did you install these bad boys?”

His smile widened. “Just this morning. I wanted to make your Christmas extra special. Do you like?” He nuzzled her breasts with his chin, raking his stubble over her nipples. “I could take them back—”

“Don’t you dare!” She clenched her fingers tightly around the leather, as Jacob shoved her legs further apart and buried his cock into her cunt. The sensation overwhelmed her and yet her body continued to demand more.

He pulled out quickly and sat up lifting her ass off the bed as he went.

Suspended in the air, arms stretched over her head, she clung to the leather straps as Jacob entered her again, slowly working her up and down his cock. Gradually, he picked up the pace to the speed and depth she craved. Julia’s tits bounced hard with each thrust. Her thighs quaked and were soon slick with her own juices, and yet he still drove into her, taking more and more from her.

One final full body orgasm raced through her quivering frame as her mind went blank. The next thing she knew, he released her from the leather straps and pulled her close. She curled up to his body and rested her head on his chest. While she listened to his heart beat slow down to its normal steady, soothing rhythm, she fought back the tears that threatened to fall. *What the hell’s wrong with me? Why can’t this be enough? Why can’t Jacob be enough?*

Chapter 13

February 12th, Present Day, Las Vegas

Eric watched Julia pace back and forth in front of the elevators for a full fifteen minutes before going over to see if he could make her feel a bit more relaxed. He couldn't let her go into her dinner meeting with his brother like this. "Julia, you're going to wear down those heels to flats, if you keep this up."

She stopped abruptly. "I don't know if I can go through with it, Eric."

He pulled her over to the stuffed chairs in the mini lounge, next to the casino floor. "Sit."

She plopped down into the cushions and gripped the armrest so tightly, her knuckles turned white. "I've never been this scared to be face to face with anyone other than my deadbeat parents. What if he doesn't want to hear me out?"

"He agreed to meet with you didn't he? That should tell you something."

"What if it's just to tell me to fuck off and stay out of his life?"

Eric chuckled. "He could have told you that already and not gone through all the trouble of seeing you at all. Besides, aren't you curious to see how he looks after all these years?" He waggled his eyebrows at her a few times and elicited a smile. "There you go. Stop thinking of the *what ifs* and just go in there and do what you came here to do. Be yourself, the Julia I got to meet today, and everything will work out."

"What if he can't forgive me?" Her voice dropped to barely a whisper but it conveyed an enormous amount of fear.

Eric's heart went out to her. "That's a chance you'll have to take. The most important thing here is you're trying to make amends. Whether or not he accepts it, isn't the point now is it?"

Julia smiled. "I never thought I'd be getting a pep talk from you."

"Never thought I'd ever see you again let alone be your cheerleader, but here we are."

"It must be the magic of Vegas." Julia winked and stood up from the chair seemingly ready to face Jacob and Quinn.

Eric stood, took her hand, and squeezed it tightly. "Must be. Would you like an escort to the restaurant, or do you think you can get there on your own?"

She slipped her arm through his and sighed. "If you could just help me get through the casino floor and to the restaurant without falling on my ass, or chickening out at the last minute, I'll be forever in your debt."

He laughed. "Stick with me. I'll get you to the restaurant with plenty of time to spare so you can check out their menu. The food there will knock your socks off. Steve's already sent word to be sure the three of you have whatever you want on the House."

Julia opened her mouth to protest.

Eric cut her off. “There’s no arguing about it. Jake and Quinn will attest to that. It’s just best to let him do this for you. He takes care of his friends and family and since you’ve agreed to take the job, you’re now part of his circle.”

“If you’re not careful Eric Hartley, I just might think you’re starting to like me.”

“Who says I’m careful?” He patted her hand and winked. “I’m glad you’re here, Julia. It’s time you and Jacob put all of this behind you, once and for all.”

* * * *

The Maître d’ escorted Julia to a quiet table, away from the majority of the dinner guests. “I hope this is satisfactory. Mr. Hartley had asked for one of our private tables.”

“Yes. This is the perfect spot.” Julia’s hands shook a bit as he helped her with her chair. “I’m afraid I’m a little early, but I couldn’t stay in my room any longer. I’m a bundle of nerves.”

“Allow me to bring you something from the bar while you wait. I’m sure Mr. and Mrs. Hartley will be here any moment.”

Julia smiled. “If you make it a double anything, I would be forever grateful.”

He bowed slightly and left her alone to go over the impressive menu.

Eric said this place had marvelous food, but I'm not sure my stomach could handle much at the moment. I'll just wait and see how the drink settles. She glanced toward the bar to see if her cocktail was on its way and immediately felt a jolt throughout her body. Her gaze locked with a set of gorgeous blue eyes. It immediately transported her back in time.

There in front of her stood Jacob, but an even more handsome version than she remembered. His light brown hair was long and tied back with a leather thong. He looked dashing as ever in the smoky gray pants and tailored purple dress shirt. On his arm must be his wife.

Julia was stunned by the vision before her. The woman was even more beautiful in the flesh. She smiled and stood to greet them, so happy and relieved to see them finally standing there in front of her. "Thank you both for coming."

The three of them stared at each other for a beat or two.

Julia giggled softly. "Where are my manners? I'm so glad both of you agreed to meet me here in Vegas. You must be Quinn. The portrait of you in Saints and Sinners really captures your beauty." She shook first Quinn's hand and then gripped Jacob's firmly with both of her hands, surprised to feel his were shaking as badly as her own. Relief washed through her as she felt the reassuring squeeze he returned to her. "This means a great deal to me you've come. Please, have a seat."

After helping Quinn get settled, Jacob sat down next to her. "I wasn't sure it was a good idea, but my wife convinced me it was time we were face to face again."

Julia felt her eyes fill again with tears. She'd been determined to hold them back, even if just for a few more minutes. She wanted to get her story out before she turned into a blubbering idiot in the restaurant. "I agree with her. It's definitely the right time for us to see each other. I have a confession though. I've been terrified of this moment for the last few years. I know now what I did to you was beyond reprehensible."

"Why do you think it's necessary for us to go through all of that pain again? Can't we just let it go and move on? It's worked for me so far." Jacob shifted a bit in his seat and smiled at Quinn. "Okay, maybe not so good up until a few years ago."

All three of them laughed and appeared to relax a little bit more. One of the waiters brought over their drinks and a few of the specialty appetizers.

"I don't mean to belittle your need to make amends, but I'm having a hard time seeing how I can help you."

Julia nodded but instead of answering him right away, she looked to Quinn. "What about you? How do you feel about meeting me? I'm sure Jake's filled you in our past together. You must think I'm a grade A bitch."

"Honestly, I'm not the best person to judge what you did or didn't do in your past. I do believe everyone deserves a second or even a third chance at happiness. From your girlfriend's letter, it seems you've been working very hard at finding your happily ever after."

"I have. It's taken a lot of years of therapy to go through all the crap in my life to find out why I did the things I did. It all comes down to allowing the walls I put up as a kid to come tumbling down. I finally accepted there were people in the world who could actually care about me for me, and not what they could get out of me. Jake was the one who originally showed me that."

Jacob stared at her a moment. All the color drained from his handsome face. "Then why did you push me away? I did everything you wanted me to do and still—it wasn't enough." He reached for Quinn's hand, gripping it hard. He swallowed a few times and then continued, "Why did you tear my heart out and crush my spirit?"

Julia bit her lower lip and wiped the now free flowing tears from her face with her napkin. This is what she came here to do. She needed to come clean and tell him every single sordid detail. If she didn't get it out now, she never would. "Because I could."

* * * *

Chapter 14

December 22nd, Thirteen years ago, Los Angeles

Everything seemed to be unraveling. If she would've just stuck with her plan to spend a few days with Carmen to clear her head, none of this would be happening right now. She wouldn't be following Jacob's motorcycle through the rain to see who'd begged him to meet at the bar near the hospital.

Actually, Julia had a pretty damn good idea of who it might be.

Earlier in the week, she'd made a huge mistake by stopping in to see Mario at the hospital. Her intentions were to break it off with him once and for all, but the old demon inside of her raised its ugly head, telling her to get one last adrenaline rush by fucking him in the supply closet.

The man had actually begged to pound her pussy one last time. Too busy pinning her against the wall and burying his condom covered dick inside her, Mario didn't seem to notice the adorable nurse in the room with them.

Poor Kathy appeared rooted right to the spot and seemed completely unable to tear her eyes away from them.

Julia's cunt clenched uncontrollably while she knew they were being watched.

Of course, Mario thought it'd been due to his sloppy fucking.

She didn't tell him his girlfriend saw their tryst, but knew it would be only a matter of time before it all came out. Of course, she'd thought she would have a little more time before Jacob found out.

Kathy seemed to be too good of a person to *not* tell him what she saw. The two of them developed quite the friendship, because of Julia's frequent trips to the emergency room.

Now here she went, ducking into a crowded bar, three days before Christmas. She watched her current boyfriend make his way through the tables to a booth near the back.

A shell shocked Kathy beckoned for him to join her and then took a huge gulp from the beer in front of her.

Julia slipped onto a seat at the bar, keeping herself hidden from them, while still able to see them clearly. She needed a drink herself to help build up the courage to go over there and pretend she'd just happened to run into them.

"What are you doing here, Julia? I thought you were getting ready to spend the next week with the Hartley clan for Christmas?" Mario stood over her, reeking of his current favorite cologne.

I wonder which one of his female patients gave him that cheap shit. "It's none of your business. I told you the last time I saw you, we were over. There's nothing left to say to each other." Julia gulped down the last of the four whiskey shots in front of her and signaled the bartender for another round. "Why don't you find one of the other broads you're fucking and see if they're in need of your companionship? I'm not in the mood for any more of your antics."

"I'm still not buying you want to break things off with me to devote yourself to that goody two shoes. Jake's not the one for you. I am. It's always been me and you know it."

Julia glanced over in time to see Kathy burst into tears and a red faced Jacob clenching his fists. *He knows. Jake knows and I've lost him forever. All because I couldn't trust the one man who ever loved me unconditionally.* "Leave me alone, Mario. I'm not settling down with anyone. Not now. Not ever."

"I'm just saying we're good together. Both of our careers can benefit from a partnership between us. I need a strong woman by my side and one whose sexual appetites rival my own."

"Good luck with that. I'm not available."

Jacob signaled to the waitress for another pitcher of beer.

Julia took that as her cue to leave. Tossing a couple bills onto the bar next to the shots the bartender just filled, she wrenched her body away from Mario so she could make her escape. She'd been able to easily hop off the stool, but when twisted her ankle as her heels came down on the wet bar floor.

Mario caught her before she fell flat on her ass.

The smell of his cologne churned her stomach and she struggled to free herself from his grasp.

"Come on, honey let me get you home safely." He tightened his grip around her waist, making it difficult for her to move away from him in the crowded bar.

"I can get my own cab, thank you. Now let me go."

"Do you really think I'd let you go alone like this? Let me get you home safe and then I'll leave you to whatever you have planned for the night."

Julia rolled her eyes knowing full well, he wouldn't just drop her off at her door. "Suit yourself, but my mind's made up."

He kept a firm grip on her arm as he hailed a cab. *There he goes again, trying to take control and show me how much he thinks I need him. It's all bullshit.* She didn't need anyone or anything more tonight, other than a hot bath and a couple more shots of whiskey to dull the pain.

He let go of her long enough for her to slide into the back seat of the cab, but slipped in next to her too fast for her to open the opposite door to make her escape.

Fuck it. If Mario wanted to foot the bill for the cab fare, she'd let him. It didn't mean she had to listen to him prattle on and on as they made it across town through the rain slicked streets. Instead, she turned inward and tuned out everything around her.

Julia had every intention of stopping Mario at the door and refusing to let him inside, but the scene at the bar played over and over in her mind on the drive over. Seeing Jacob talk to Kathy, and guessing the words she used to describe what she saw in the supply closet, made her sick to her stomach. *How did things go so wrong, so fast? Why couldn't I just be happy with Jake and forget everyone else?* The look of shock and disbelief on his face would haunt her in her dreams and she couldn't handle it right now.

Mario insisted he go up with her to be sure she got to her door without passing out in the elevator. He took her silence as permission to take her arm again.

By the time they reached her floor, she was in no condition to argue with him. So, instead of facing the empty condo she shared with Jacob, Julia allowed Mario inside.

He helped her out of her wet jacket and shoes, careful not to twist her now swollen ankle as he assisted her over to her couch. All the while, he plied her with soothing words she knew didn't mean shit. He played her like the rest of the broads he fucked.

What the hell? She put the walls up around her heart again and turned on the personality she knew would enjoy `play time' with Mario. The one devastated over hurting Jacob could just curl up in the corner alone and cry for a bit before having to face the music and admit she'd fucked up yet again.

* * * *

Chapter 15

He wasn't going there to confront her. Really, he wasn't. Jacob just wanted to get his bags and head out early to see his family. He needed to be away from her and think things through. Still, something in the back of his mind told him he wanted to hear it directly from her mouth. Until that was done, it just didn't seem real to him. How could Julia make him give up everything, including time with his family if she didn't love him? Was it all some twisted game? Was he just a new toy she would toss away as soon as something better came along?

His mind wouldn't stop with the questions, even after the pitcher of beer he shared with Kathy over the last several hours. He made sure to put her safely in a cab before he finally left the bar and headed back to what he once thought of as home.

The rain was really coming down by the time he pulled his motor cycle into the garage of their building. His teeth chattered and he felt chilled to the bone. Jacob's clothes were drenched and clung to his skin. He definitely needed a hot shower before he finished packing for his trip to see his family. Maybe he should just spend the night in a hotel and drive in the morning when the weather was better? Anywhere, but their condo would suit him just fine.

The sound of music filled his ears as soon as he opened the door. The lights were all dimmed in the living room, but it wasn't too dark to prevent him from seeing pieces of men's clothing on the floor near the couch. The hallway leading toward the master bedroom was lined with candles and a few more garments he recognized as Julia's lingerie. In fact, they were part of the set he'd given her for her birthday four months ago. His stomach churned with each step he took down the corridor. The bitter taste of his own bile filled his mouth when he finally reached his destination. The door to the bedroom only sat open a few inches, but the space seemed to be all he needed in order to see and hear everything.

Any thoughts he'd entertained about his relationship with Julia continuing completely left his mind the instant he peered into the room. There they were on the bed he built with his own two hands.

Julia faced the doorway, her eyes closed, and her arms braced behind her on her lover's abs as she plunged up and down an enormous cock.

Neither one of them noticed Jacob standing there in disbelief, dripping rain water on the thick, white carpet.

"Baby, your pussy is all I ever think about. I love the way you ride my cock!"

I know that voice! She's fucking him right here in our bed! Jacob tried to speak but the words wouldn't come out. His throat seized up, barely allowing him to breathe. This might just be one of his worst nightmares come to life. He couldn't move or close his eyes to the scene playing out in front of him.

* * * *

Julia's body was no longer under her control. She didn't want to feel anything anymore. She didn't want to feel the pain anymore. She screwed up her life yet again, all because she couldn't keep her legs closed. She'd found a man who loved her unconditionally and yet she did everything in her power to push him away. *How could anyone love someone like her, out of control and damaged beyond repair?* Men and women like Mario were the kind she'd been drawn to like a mouth to a flame. Unfortunately, the release she so desperately craved never came from these encounters. She needed to lose herself completely to find it.

Riding Mario's cock with her eyes closed, she tried to put herself into another world, one where no one else existed except her and the one who she truly loved with all her heart and soul. Unfortunately, the one she was with at the moment didn't fit the bill. She convinced herself she was the one in control, when all along she'd let herself be manipulated by another. No more.

Slowly, she opened her eyes. Standing there in the doorway was the one man who never treated her like shit. He wore a look of shock and disbelief on his face, along with something more. *I've ripped his heart out of his chest and he's still there, trying to figure out a way to make us work. No more. I can't let him give up any more of his life for me. I'm not worth it.* She picked up the pace and fucked Mario with wild abandon, tossing her head and hair around to cover her face. She screamed out as her body ripped through another orgasm. She steeled herself for the now inevitable confrontation.

Jacob swiftly crossed the room and pulled Julia from the bed.

Mario bellowed his protest at the sudden motion of her being removed from his dick, but froze once he made eye contact with Jacob.

"Don't you fucking move, Carlos."

"Let her go, Hartley. It's been over between the two of you for some time now. She doesn't want anything to do with you or your family."

Julia bit her lip as Jacob turned back toward her. Her hand rested on his chest to keep her balance and she felt his heart beating wildly under her fingertips.

He searched her eyes, looking for answers that just weren't there. "Is it true?"

She giggled and then laughed outright before she could stop herself. All of the stress of the last few months finally caught up with her. The phone call from her mother, the gallery opening, Mario not allowing her to walk away, the pain in Jacob's eyes as he basically begged her for some answer as to why she ruined their life together—all of it finally broke her hold on reality. She needed to push Jacob away for good. It was the only way to save him. "God, what does it take for you to get the hint? I don't need you anymore. The gallery opening was a success. I'll be busy for the next year, creating new pieces from all the commissions generated by the opening. I do have you to thank for that, Jake but eventually I'll need a new muse. It was fun while it lasted but it's time for you to move on, baby. It's better this way. Trust me."

Mario attempted to get up from the bed but seemed to be tangled up in the sheets. All he could manage was a slight crawl toward the end of the bed, and closer to Jacob—a big mistake.

Before Julia's mind could comprehend what happened, Jacob swung and hit the doctor in the jaw with his helmet. The loud crack reverberated throughout the room it could've been the helmet or Mario's jaw, but she didn't care.

Mario appeared to be out cold.

Julia saw her chance to get Jacob to leave her forever. "Get the fuck out of here, Jake!" Julia put on her best angry act and yanked her arm from his grip. She stood her ground between him and Mario, but didn't move a muscle to help her naked and unconscious lover. It took all she had to stay still. The booze she'd taken in throughout the night made her dizzy and the pain in her swollen ankle bordered on unbearable.

"As always, you get what you want, Julia and to hell with anyone who gets in your way. This time, you've gone too far. One day, you'll find yourself all alone, with no one there to be your muse or your doormat." Jacob stormed out of the condo and Julia's life.

He'd left her to clean up the mess she'd made of everything all by herself. When she heard the front door slam, she collapsed into a heap on the floor and sobbed.

* * * *

Chapter 16

Julia attempted to focus as cold fury swept through her body. Her hands shook as she grabbed more ice from the freezer to wrap in a clean towel. Mario already ruined two of them while washing his bloody face. Alone, the ruined towels wouldn't have made her blow her top. It'd been the tears she couldn't control that sent her blood beyond its boiling point. *How could I let any man get under my skin this way? Jake's better off without me in his life. I'd only make him miserable. Better he leaves hating me now, than a few years down the road.*

"You know, this would have been a hell of a lot easier on everyone if you would've said goodbye to him before now." Mario examined his reflection closely. His already black and blue jawline looked swollen to nearly twice the normal size. He turned to take the ice she offered and snorted. "Tears? Really?"

Julia's face flushed scarlet. She ground her teeth together and glared. "Don't you dare! Jacob meant the world to me."

"As your muse. Yeah, so you keep saying." The doctor winced as he moved his jaw side to side then rubbed the fresh ice over it. "I think that fucker broke my jaw!"

Julia glared at him through the mirror. "You should be thankful that's all he did to you, asshole. I'm tired of you making fun of my work. You know goddamn well I was blocked for such a long time. I couldn't create one decent sculpture or painting for anyone until he came into my life."

"So, why the hell did you keep *this* going between us? If he meant so much to you, why keep taking the risk he'd catch us?"

She stormed out of the master bathroom and straight to the bar in the living room to pour a double shot of whisky. She didn't bother to reach for the fancy crystal decanter, but went straight for the bottle.

Mario followed hot on her heels, still naked, his once engorged cock shriveled down to the size of a limp egg noodle.

Normally, she'd laugh at such a sight, but not now. She remained too pissed. "I could ask you the same thing! What about that adorable nurse Kathy you've been stringing along? She was there in the supply closet watching you fuck me against the wall with your scrubs down around your ankles!"

Now it seemed to be his turn to be flustered. "You *knew* she was there?"

Julia's stomach fluttered seeing the shocked look on her lover's face. It was so worth it seeing him this way, under her control again. The way she'd wanted all of her lover's to be—except Jacob. "Of course I did. You kept telling me it was over between the two of you. Well, I just made sure of it." She tossed back the rest of her drink and reached for the bottle to fill her glass again.

"All these years we've been doing this, I've put up with your moods, your multiple lovers and all the other crap, because you always came back to me. Once

Hartley entered the picture, you pushed me aside. You've had *him* all this time. Was I supposed to be at your beck and call in an empty bed while you fucked him?"

Julia threw her half full glass at his head. The whisky coated the wall behind him, but missed Mario by only a few inches. "Yes! We had an *understanding*, Dr. Carlos, not a relationship. No one can fuck you like I do, and I'll be damned if I play second to anyone, not even someone as delicious as Kathy." She grabbed the whiskey bottle and brought it to her lips. The liquor burned her throat going down, but she didn't care. She just wanted to dull the pain and make everything disappear for a while. *Damn him. Damn Mario to hell for fucking everything up!*

"That's where you're wrong, mi amor. You can't keep playing our game the way you wanted to. The rules changed as soon as you let Jake into your bed and your heart. You got more than you bargained for with him." Mario waited a few beats before he continued in a soft, subdued voice, "You fell in love with him. Why else would you hang on for so long? You've had at least a dozen lovers since we first started. Not one ever kept you in their bed longer than a few weeks, except me...and *him.*

Julia's heart pounded and the room appeared to spin in front of her eyes. "No. I don't need any of you, other than to satisfy an itch now and then so I can keep creating my art. Fell in love with him? You don't know what the fuck you're talking about."

"Is that so? Why were you packing your bags to go with him to visit his family if you just need him to satisfy an itch? You cleared your schedule for an entire week. That's so unlike you."

"How do you know about that?" Julia's mind raced. She didn't remember telling him about the trip to San Diego. "I needed to travel for a few of my commissions over the next couple of weeks. I told you that last week. Whatever gave you the idea I was planning on spending the holidays with Jake's family?"

Mario laughed in her face. "Do you think I don't have my own sources about you? Your hot little assistant, Darla spilled it. She couldn't keep her mouth shut after I bent her over your desk and slammed my dick into her for over an hour. I don't think she walked normally all week. She *loves* to suck cock. You should try it some time."

"Fuck you." *Thank God, he doesn't know the real reason I packed my bags. I wasn't rushing off to meet Jacob's family. I was running away from them. What does it matter now what Darla told him?* She made a mental note to fire the little cunt as soon as she came back from her vacation. *Hell, why wait.* Julia picked up her cell phone and activated the speed dial. "Darla? Are you enjoying your vacation so far? That's fantastic, because I just found out you can't keep your mouth or your legs shut. Don't bother coming back to the gallery. Your kinds of services are no longer needed." She slammed the phone down on top of the bar. "Are you happy now, Mario?"

He shook his head and sighed. "Not really. The three of us could've had a lot more fun together with her sucking my cock and you eating out her pussy. Now that's something I would've paid money to do, but no. You saved all of the fun for your muse."

Julia finally had enough of the man standing in front of her. She should have cut him loose ages ago. All the drama he created wasn't what she wanted from him at all. He always tried to control her in some way and it'd gotten worse with each passing year. Enough was enough. She took another swig of the whisky and simply stared at him. She did her best to keep her face neutral, but she felt so tired and knew it showed in her eyes. She fought the urge to slap the smug smile off his face while she waited for Mario to explain. "What the hell are you talking about?"

"Darla showed me the tapes starring the three of you. You sure you want to give up that piece of ass?"

"Jacob's gone. Why dwell on that now? The threesome was his idea, not mine. Darla was always drooling over him, more than eager to agree when we approached her about it." Julia waved her hand in the air, dismissing any further discussion.

Mario wouldn't let it go. "Really? Darla said you'd been fucking her for over a year before she hopped into bed with you and Hartley."

"Enough! This is exactly why she's no longer in my employ or in my bed. If you don't watch it, you'll find yourself in the same boat!"

Mario crossed the room so fast; Julia didn't register it until his fingers were clamped on her bare upper arms.

He shook her, causing her to lose her tenuous grip on the bottle of whiskey, sending it crashing to the floor. He sneered, "Don't threaten me, Julia. I'm not one of your employees and I'm not like Hartley. I *will* strike a woman."

Maybe it'd been the whiskey, or maybe she just didn't care anymore, but right then she wished he would get on with it. From her sick bastard of a stepfather to the self-important Dr. Carlos, they only wanted one thing from her. However, when they didn't get their way, they got violent. *Fuck it. I'm tired of running and tired of hiding.* Julia held Mario's gaze, daring him to live up to her expectations. "Go ahead. Why should you be any different than the other men in my life? The only man who *ever* treated me with kindness, respect and love was Jacob."

He loosened his grip on her arms for a split second.

She pulled away and retreated, steering clear of the broken glass to stand near the couch. "He told me he wanted to spend the rest of his life with me. No one has ever said that to me and meant it. He did and I drove him away."

Mario's shoulders fell and he closed his eyes. "I love you, Julia. I've told you that repeatedly over the last couple of years."

She shook her head and laughed. "No, you love the idea of us together and fucking all the time. You love the idea of a famous artist on your arm. It's all about image with you, *your* image that is. You don't give a shit about anyone or anything but yourself and your almighty career. You haven't got a clue what love is. If anything, you're madly in love with the image you've created for yourself."

Mario stared at her, eyes wide and looking absolutely clueless.

Oh my God! Everything I accused Mario of doing, I've done myself. The character of Julia Santos is more important to me than anyone, more than Jake, more than myself. I can't keep doing this. It all became abundantly clear to her. She knew if she wanted her life to get better it needed to start with the half-naked man in front of her.

He stood while still staring at her.

She sighed loudly and crossed her arms over her chest. "Just cut the bullshit, Mario. You couldn't even let me enjoy my gallery opening with Jacob. You had to weasel your way into every conversation I had with my clients. Do you think your behavior wasn't noticed? Instead of focusing on my art, people were watching *you*. Did you ever think maybe your actions would cost me a potential sale?"

Mario rolled his eyes. "Stop being so melodramatic, Julia. There are more important things in life than selling a few pieces of your *so called* art. You'd know that if you would just agree to be my wife. I can give you everything your heart desires."

She laughed in his face. "And what would that be? You've never taken any time to find out what makes me tick or what would make me happy. Jake did. The threesome with Darla was his idea whether you want to believe it or not. That beautiful bed we were screwing in? He made that himself after I told him about my fantasy of sleeping in a bed like that with those red sheers, making love for days on end with him. She sat hard onto the couch and sobbed.

Mario eased down next to her and wrapped his arms around her shaking body, and rocked her gently. "All of that isn't you, mi amor."

She pushed him away. "It could be. It's who I've always wanted to be, but no one has ever given me the chance."

He took her hands into his, tightly squeezing them. "You're kidding yourself. You're not the love sick puppy dog type like Kathy. You're a strong, independent diva through and through. You *take* what you want when you want it and the hell with the consequences. So do I. That's why we belong together."

Julia pulled her hands away, leaned back into the cushions, and tucked her legs under herself. "Don't be an idiot, Mario. We can't go on this way, any more than I could with Jacob."

"Why the hell not?" He flopped back on the couch cushions, exhaled loudly and glared at her. His entire demeanor reminded Julia of a spoiled child being told no by his parents in a toy store. The kind of look that warned you if you didn't give him what he wanted, a temper tantrum was soon to follow. At this point, she could care less.

He wanted to know why? Well, he was going to get it with both barrels.

"Honestly, you bore me. It was the chase with you, the thrill of being caught that attracted me to you. The fact you jumped every single time I snapped my fingers appealed to me. Not anymore. Now there is just...you. *Nothing* about you appeals to me anymore. Is that plain enough for you or do you need a flow chart?"

Mario's face drained of all color and he looked absolutely stunned.

Julia didn't understand why he just couldn't get the hint.

Instead, he seemed to be struggling for words.

Now the real Dr. Carlos finally appeared and she couldn't stand the sight of him anymore.

"Having sex in every public place imaginable, no longer turns you on? Ten years of hiding in closets and sneaking around is not enough for you? *Now* you're bored?" He grabbed his jeans and polo shirt from the floor where he'd carelessly tossed them earlier that evening. "I think it's time I head over to the hospital to have my jaw x-rayed. You need some alone time to think this all through."

"There's nothing to think about. You said it yourself. I want what I want when I want it. I don't want you or your dick anymore, Mario. It's over. Say hello to Kathy for me."

"Funny you should mention her. I threatened to have her fired if she so much as hinted she saw you and me together. I was trying to protect you from anymore gossip."

"Boy, you sure are full of yourself." She laughed. "Protect me? You should be more worried about yourself. You don't have that kind of power at the hospital."

"Like hell. I know the Chief of Staff personally."

"So do I, or should I say we know each other *very* intimately." She paused to let that little tidbit sink into his thick skull. "Carmen and I have been seeing each other on and off for the last twelve years. *She's* my best friend and confidant. You were never the longest fling for me and you were a fool to assume your importance in my life or at the hospital. It's not Kathy who should be afraid of losing her job. She's not the one fucking her patients." Julia had been waiting for just the right moment to spring that on him.

The Chief knew about the affair with Mario right from the beginning. Dr. Carmen Hall was the jealous type and never liked Dr. Carlos from the first day she took over the administrative duties at the hospital. If it wasn't for Julia begging to let her have fun, Carmen would've never promoted Mario to his current position.

His job meant more to him than anything, and Julia knew he'd be doing some serious damage control over the next few days in order to keep it. The thought of it made her clit throb. If she timed it right, she could find herself spread eagle on the Chief's desk with Carmen's lovely face buried in her cunt. Unfortunately, that would have to wait until she got rid of her current problem.

Mario finally finished dressing and slipped on his leather jacket. "I've done nothing but play by your rules and try to shield you from gossiping, jealous nurses. Instead of being grateful, you treat me like shit. Enough is enough. I'm tired of your threats, Julia. You're bored with me and want me out of your life?" His eyes glistened with angry tears while waited for an answer.

Julia coldly stared at him.

He backed away from her with his hands held up in front of him in surrender. “Done.” He slammed the door as he left, causing two framed paintings to fall to the tile floor.

Both were of Jacob riding his motorcycle through the rain. One of them was of a scene in the summer with a rainbow in the background and the other was at night. The frame of the night scene shattered as it hit the floor. A jagged edge of the frame sliced through the canvas, destroying Jacob’s image.

Tears spilled from her eyes again as she knelt to the floor to pick up the torn portrait. “I’m so sorry, love. Someday, you’ll find the one you’re meant to spend the rest of your life with. It’s just not me. It never was.”

* * * *

Chapter 17

Julia shuffled to the kitchen to discard the remnants of the damaged picture. It'd been one of her favorites. Jacob never posed for it. She'd done it all from memory. She loved watching him ride down the street on his motorcycle, long hair flying behind him, no helmet. He looked so alive, vibrant and happy. Now the portrait as well as their life together was ruined, damaged beyond repair.

The pain in his eyes tonight broke her heart. Against her better judgment, she'd let herself grow too attached and made him fall in love with her. Right from the start, she knew she could never be the woman to fill his heart and soul. No matter how hard she tried, she always strayed, making the excuse of boredom and the need for a thrill. Truthfully? Being loved by someone as special as Jacob scared the shit out of her, and yet, made her feel like she could really be happy if she just let her guard down all the way.

It wasn't meant to be. How could he accept the real Julia, the girl who let her parents use her as their personal sex slave until she was sixteen? Now she didn't really know who or what she wanted anymore and she was too tired of running.

Julia opened the cupboard and pulled out the bottle of pain killers Mario gave her after she sliced open her arm with the mirror shard. She'd left them behind in the drawer where she tossed them, but the doctor made sure to give the bottle to Jacob when she'd been discharged from the hospital.

Now, all thirty capsules called out to her, but she ignored them and decided on just three, chasing them down with a half glass of water from the tap. "Maybe if I just went to sleep everything will be better in the morning, or afternoon."

She shuffled back out to the living room and curled up in the afghan Carmen knitted for her years ago. The yarn still felt soft against her bare skin and smelled of her best friend. Julia smiled. Even when they weren't together, Carmen always seemed to be there to take care of her.

* * * *

"That was a bit painful to watch." Daniel turned to the Goddess Fate and shook his head. "I'm not sure I'm the best Guardian for her. She's had to put up so many barriers to protect herself from everyone, I don't know if I'll be able to get through to her."

Fate nodded. "You will. We wouldn't have assigned her to you if We didn't think you could make a difference in her current path. By interceding in Jacob and Quinn's lives now, we also have to step in for Julia. In many ways, she needs us more than all the rest. It's Jacob's accident that'll be the catalyst for change in her world. If she doesn't choose wisely, the change will not be a happy one in this lifetime." Fate smile broadly at the young angel. "Besides, my brother Lucius is very fond of her and her soul mate, Carmen. He feels you are the very best choice to watch over Julia now. I know you and your partner have a lot of humans to watch over in this group, but it's important that all of them continue on the right paths. We can't intervene with a few of them and not the others as well. It will be up to you to give the nudge she needs to find her way and more importantly, she needs to believe she deserves the happiness that awaits her."

The heavily tattooed and pierced Guardian Angel still wasn't quite convinced. "I'll have to take your word for it. I promise to do everything I can to help her, but as you said, she has to believe she deserves the blessing. Otherwise, she'll continue to make the wrong choices and relive all the pain she's suffered and caused to others over and over again."

"Speaking of that—"

"Jacob?" Daniel's jaw clenched repeatedly.

"He needs you now. Yeshua forbid me to allow Michael to be there to witness his son's accident or to protect him from the injuries he'll suffer. He never said I couldn't send others in his place." The Goddess gripped Daniel's hand tightly, projecting a bit of her own energy into the angel to combine with his. "You must go now to shield him from the beating his body will take on that road. I'll send others there to lend their strength to yours. Go."

Daniel quickly faded in front of Lady Fate's twinkling emerald eyes. She reached out and touched Julia's forehead before she too left the condo. "Sleep my child.

Those pills along with the whiskey you drank will take you near death, but I'll be here to keep you safe until your dreams are able to transport you to my Island. There you will find the answers you seek."

* * * *

Chapter 18

February 12th, Present Day, Las Vegas

By the look on Quinn's face, Julia knew her statement shocked her.

Quinn appeared to struggle to find the words she wanted to say in response. "Did you just say because you could? What the hell does that mean?"

Julia's eyes locked with Quinn's. "I did everything back then because I *could* do it. No one told me no or denied me anything. I went from being a possession and sexual play thing for my parents, to the one who had all the control. Unfortunately, I went through way too many years, thinking that way of life made me happy. In truth, it did just the opposite." Julia bolted down the rest of the scotch the waiter served her with their appetizers. She held her breath a moment to steady herself before she continued, "If I didn't drive Jake away when I did, I would've taken him down that dark path with me. I had to make him give up on me once and for all. It was the only way."

Jacob stared at her and slowly shook his head. "What do you mean the only way? I could've done without seeing you in bed with another man."

The memory of that night flooded back into her mind. The room started to spin and she clutched the table to help steady her shaking body. Julia needed to keep going. If she didn't get the whole story out now, she never would. Once again, she took a deep breath and gathered the courage up to look into her ex lover's eyes. "I'm truly sorry you saw that. I was drunk and he escorted me home. I never intended for it to happen in our condo, but it did and I can't change that. My intention that night was to find some way to avoid meeting your mother. I knew she would see right through me and know I wasn't the one you needed in your life."

"If you felt that way, why didn't you tell me? It would've hurt like hell, but I could've handled it a whole lot better than what ended up happening. Besides, I wasn't the only one who got hurt. Kathy Baker told me about the two of you that night. She was devastated finding out the man she loved was planning on marrying someone else."

Julia snorted. "I would never have agreed to marry that idiot. Mario Carlos had all sorts of grandiose plans. It was always about image with him. He ended up treating me as his possession and there was no way in hell I was going to live through that again. Kathy was so much better off without him too. He screwed anything and everything that walked into the ER."

Quinn tilted her head to the side. "I'm curious. If you didn't want any more to do with Mario, how did he end up taking you home?"

"I followed Jake to the bar."

"What?" Jacob ran his hands through his hair, loosening the band holding it in place at the nape of his neck.

More memories flashed through Julia's mind. He always rubbed his stubbly chin or used his fingers to comb through his hair when he felt shocked or confused.

"I didn't see you there." Instead of retying his long hair, he let it flow down his back.

Julia loved the look on him. "You were deep in conversation with Kathy. I took a seat at the bar, so I could watch the two of you without either one of you noticing I was there. By her facial expressions, I knew she was telling you all about watching Mario and me go at it in the supply closet. I panicked. I didn't want you to find out about any of that, at least not from anyone other than me. I knew I needed to break things off with you, but I wasn't ready. Instead of just going over there and talking to both of you, I ordered a shot of whiskey, then another and another. I had a line of them in front of me, quickly making my way through them before I noticed Mario sitting next to me, ordering me yet another round of shots. I made it completely through two rounds, then ordered a third while you and Kathy were still talking to each other."

"So, Mario offered to drive you home and fuck you in our bed?"

"Jake!" Quinn squeezed his upper arm slightly. "Let her finish."

"It's a fair question, Quinn. I didn't start out with that in mind. In fact, I fought with him about it. I didn't want anything more to do with him and told him as much, but when I tried to leave, I was a bit unsteady on my feet. He caught me before I fell on my ass, but not before I twisted the shit out of my ankle. Then, he insisted he wasn't going to allow me to leave in my condition. He wanted to make sure to get me home safe and sound. He knew if I drank enough, my *hell no* just might turn into a maybe. I thought if I drank enough, I would have the courage to let you go, not to sleep with him. It'd been the furthest thing on my mind while still in the bar. I completely zoned out on him during the cab ride, but he didn't seem to care. When I got home, all I could see was the hurt on your face when Kathy told you about what I'd done. I couldn't bear it. So, I just shut down."

"Did you ever love me, Julia or was it all just a game?" Jacob's voice came out as barely a whisper.

This was what she'd been most afraid of admitting to him even after all these years. Seeing him there next to Quinn, she knew it was finally the time to confess that last bit to him. He needed to know as much as she needed to tell him.

"I did care for you deeply. Was it love? Yes, but was I in love with you? No. I tried to mold you into someone you weren't. You don't do that to someone who has your heart. It was and has always been Carmen. It took your accident to make me see that. If we stayed together, I would've made you miserable. The fact remains if I didn't cut you out of my life, you wouldn't have found Quinn. I was never the one for you, Jake. I knew that then, and now. Seeing the two of you together tonight proves my point."

"So, we're right back to my original question. Why did we have to rehash all of this again? I nearly died in that accident. I spent years in rehab healing physically and mentally. I almost lost my chance to be with Quinn because of everything I went through with you. I managed to get through all of it *because* of her. I don't want to relive all the misery again. Not now. Not ever."

The waiter arrived with their dinners before Julia could answer.

Quinn watched the both of them and appeared to want to say something, but she too held her tongue. Her eyes widened and filled with sympathy.

Her expression was enough to help Julia answer Jacob. For a fleeting moment she wished she'd waited to meet with them until Carmen could be there to support her as Quinn was there for Jacob. It definitely was long past time to tell him the rest. "In order for me to move forward in my life, it was important for me to tell you face to face what happened and why. I had to tell you I'm sorry for hurting you. Because you did love me the way you did, I was able to realize I didn't have to run away from my past any longer. I didn't need to hide behind a made up persona. I could just be myself and not be the center of attention all the time. Because of your accident, I figured out what and who was really important to me. It was time I stopped running from the horrors of my childhood and finally put them to rest. It's taken all these years and one hell of a patient therapist to get me to this point today. I couldn't give my whole heart to anyone else, especially Carmen, until I saw you again and asked if you could ever forgive me."

Jacob visibly relaxed and closed his eyes. "I forgave you a long time ago. Maybe it's time you finally forgive yourself and be happy with Carmen."

Quinn smiled at her husband and then reached across the table to hold Julia's hands in her own. "We could tell from her letter, Carmen has loved you for a very long time."

Julia smiled brightly. "It's over twenty-five years now she's been by my side, allowing me to work through everything and find myself. She's the one who's always had my heart. I just didn't know it then, but I do now. I was never one of those people who believed in soul mates or love at first sight. Hell, I thought it was just something in romance novels. Seeing the two of you together tonight, has given me a renewed hope for the future. How did the two of you meet by the way?"

Jacob smiled broadly for the first time that evening. "I'm not sure you'd believe our story if we told you."

"Oh, I don't know Jake. You'd be surprised by what I believe in nowadays."

* * * *

Chapter 19

Thirteen Years Ago, the Island

Julia awakened to the sound of waves crashing on a beach. She opened her eyes to find she wasn't on her couch but in a king sized four poster bed, covered in pale pink material that gently tossed in the breeze coming through the screen door in front of her. "Where the hell am I?" She sat up in the bed and continued to take in her surroundings. At the end of the bed, Julia noted a white silk robe and matching slippers on the floor. The closet doors were open revealing several colorful dresses and matching sandals.

She tossed the covers aside to find she was completely naked. That in itself wasn't unusual for her, but she distinctly remembered falling asleep on the couch in her condo, wrapped up in an afghan. The closet temporarily forgotten, she frantically searched through the comforter and sheets, terrified to be without the one thing that offered her comfort and security when she felt alone. Julia breathed a sigh of relief when she noticed the blanket folded neatly on the dressing table next to the bed. She smiled and chastised herself for panicking. She looked around again for any clues as to how she got there. "Hello? Is anyone here?"

She slipped into the robe then explored a bit further into what she assumed was a bungalow of some sort. She found a fully stocked kitchen and pantry; a living room with an entertainment center, a huge bathroom with a glass enclosed two person shower, and sunken spa tub. The one thing she didn't find was a telephone. She smiled. If she couldn't call out, then no one could call in.

Rushing back to the bedroom while dropping the robe on the floor she then flipped through the sun dresses hanging in the closet. She picked out a red halter dress and decided to pass on the sandals. She wanted to walk barefoot on the beach, something she hadn't done for far too long. If this all was just a dream, she wanted to enjoy every single minute of it before she woke up in the city again.

The only way to the beach seemed to be through the sliding doors on the other side of the bedroom. The sound of sea gulls reached her ears as she stepped out onto the deck. A bubbling hot tub sat to her left and to her right was an outdoor kitchen, complete with a grill pit and cushioned deck chairs. Directly in front of her stretched the pale sandy beach. The waves called to her and she practically ran through the sand to get to the point where the water gently lapped against her calves. Julia wiggled her toes into the sand, loving the feel of it slipping and sliding between them. "This is sheer Heaven."

Then it hit her. The whole confrontation with Jacob and Mario in the condo replayed on fast forward in her mind. She remembered drinking way too much whiskey and then swallowing some pain killers. "Oh, my God! I just wanted to sleep. I didn't want to die. This is why I'm here. I'm dead." She sank to her knees in the surf and sobbed.

"Julia, you're not dead." A tall blond man stood before her on the beach. He looked to be in his late twenties, covered in tattoos and sporting multiple piercings. His eyes were what drew her right in. They were the blue green color of the ocean she sat in. His eyes made her feel immediately at ease.

He held out his hand to her. "Come on. We've a lot to talk about and I'm sure you're full of questions for me too."

"Where did you come from? I thought I was the only one here." Julia took his hand and allowed him to help her get to her feet and out of the water. Goosebumps covered her body, but she wasn't cold. "If I'm not dead, then how did I get here?"

He laughed. "I'll answer all your questions, but first you have to give me a chance to do it before you fire off more." He wrapped a large beach towel around her shoulders as they made their way back up toward her bungalow. "I've been waiting for you to wake up. I'm the Guardian assigned to watch over you and help you find your way back to the destiny chosen for you by The Three."

She sat down on one of the deck chairs and beckoned to him to sit next to her. "Guardian? As in *guardian angel*?"

He nodded. "My name is Daniel. The Goddess Fate chose me to watch over you and several other people. One of them you know already, Jake Hartley."

Julia's eyes filled with tears. "I hurt him so badly. Is he okay? I mean he stormed out of our condo last night. I don't know where he went."

Daniel shook his head. "He was in a horrific accident on his bike. He slammed into the back of a semi—"

"No! He's not dead. He can't be." Julia bolted out of her chair and barely reached the end of the deck before she threw up.

Daniel went immediately to her side, holding her hair out of the way until she stopped retching. "I'm not going to sugar coat it for you, Julia. Jake's fighting for his life right now. But you need to believe me when I tell you he's in good hands. His father is my partner and right now he's there with him and the rest of the family."

"He wouldn't be there if it wasn't for me. I did this to him." Sobs tore through her body again. She'd never cried over anyone or anything before Jacob. All of it became more than she could take. "Please. Leave me here to die. Take care of him."

The Guardian wrapped his muscled arms around her and held her against his chest. "That's not why you're here. In fact, you've been allowed to come here in order for your heart and soul to mend. Then, you have to make a choice."

Julia wiped the tears from her face and gazed into Daniel's eyes. "I don't understand. What is this place?"

"We call it The Island. Basically, it's what humans would call limbo. It's the realm between life and death. The ability to come here is a gift given to you by Yeshua, Fate, and Lucius. You have to choose to either stay here and wait until your next life cycle, or go back to face your demons and fight for your chance to be with your soul mate and your chosen destiny."

"The only person that's ever loved me like that, the only one who told me he loved me and wanted to spend the rest of his life with me, is fighting for his life in a hospital bed." Julia managed to get back into the deck chair without having another wave of nausea hit. She curled up in the towel again and wondered if it would be the best thing to stay here and not go back to all the pain she'd caused.

Daniel smiled. "The only one? Think hard. Who's been by your side through everything? Who has let you pursue all your desires and still loves you unconditionally?"

She smiled through her tears. "But Carmen can't be my soul mate. It's one thing to have an affair, but the love we have for each other will never be accepted, especially not in her world as a doctor and hospital administrator. The religious groups in L.A. would crucify her if our relationship was made public. The hospital Board wouldn't want to have that kind of publicity. Carmen's worked too hard to get where she's at in her career. I won't be responsible for ruining another person's life."

"I understand your fears about that, but you and all those groups have it completely wrong. The Three didn't create us as just male or female. We are both. Soul mates are just that, mates of the soul. Being a male or female isn't part of it. Souls have no gender. They're just pure life force."

Julia shook her head. "That may very well be true, but after all I've done in my life I don't deserve to have that kind of happiness. Jacob does. Carmen does. But not me."

Daniel took her hands into his calloused ones. "Why not? If The Three feel you're worthy, who are you or anyone to judge differently?"

"I'm scared, Daniel. What if I've gone too far in my life to turn things around? I don't think I can face the ugliness in my past, let alone ask Carmen to stand by my side when I do it. It's not fair to her. It's best I just stay away. I've made a mess out of enough lives."

"I can't force you to go back, but you have to understand this. If you choose to stay here, you will in fact die in the Earth Realm. Everything in that life will be gone and all you'll know is right here on this island until you next life cycle begins. You won't remember anything from the life you've led up until now. Within hours of your choice to not go back, those memories will be locked away. All the happy times will be gone. Carmen's life will never be the same after losing you. You can't change what's already happened, but you can choose to accept this second chance you've been given."

"Can I take a day or two to think it over?" Julia's mind raced. She needed some time to sort through everything before she made her decision. For once in her life, she needed to not act on impulse.

The Guardian nodded. "The Goddess and I will come for your answer in a couple days. Until then, make yourself at home here in your bungalow. There are others on this island paradise, but you won't be able to see them unless you decide to stay here."

"Jacob's here, isn't he?"

Daniel nodded. He's been given the same opportunity, but his choice is much harder to make."

"Why? I would think he'd jump at the chance to find his soul mate."

"He does find her here on the Island. They must choose to go back and find each other later in their lives, or stay here and wait for their next rebirth."

"Hell, if he can be here with his heart and soul, why would he ever want to go back?" Julia thought that choice would be the easiest one to make. She could live here forever with Carmen. With no outside influences to come between them, their life together would actually be paradise.

"Too many other lives hang in the balance with those two, including yours. Their lives intersect with so many. If they stay here, the futures of the others would be forever altered in this lifetime. People have to continue to be reborn and live their lives over and over again, until they learn all the lessons needed to achieve their chosen destinies."

"So, if I give up on this one, I'll have to continue on to another life cycle again and again until I get it right? The painful parts could happen all over again?"

Daniel stared at her a moment, then answered, "Yes. You may be born into a family that doesn't abuse you, but a family friend or stranger may be the one. You may never have to go through that pain again, but I can't guarantee that any more than I can tell you you'll find

Carmen right away in the next life. You're given the chance for your happily ever after now as long as you're willing to fight for it."

Julia closed her eyes and bit her lower lip. "Okay. I'll think it all over and have an answer for you when you return. If I have any other questions about anything, how do I contact you?"

He smiled as he stood in front of her. "All you have to do is call. I'll be right here when you need me. I promise." Daniel waved as he faded right in front of her eyes. "Listen to your heart, Julia. It will never steer you wrong."

* * * *

"How can I be sure it will be the right choice?" Julia's eyes snapped open to find herself back in her condo, wrapped in Carmen's afghan. "Whoa, that was one hell of a dream."

She looked around the room and sighed deeply as the visions of what happened there the night before came flooding back. "I wish I could chalk the rest of it up to my overactive imagination."

She stood up carefully, trying not to put too much weight on her injured ankle only to find the pain completely gone. She shifted her weight from foot to foot to test it out, and sure enough both ankles were sound. Keeping the blanket wrapped around her body, Julia slowly made her way back to her bedroom, surveying the damage and avoiding the broken glass on the floor as she went.

The candles she and Mario lit the night before were completely burned down and melted wax caked the table tops the holders sat upon. She spotted her purse in the middle of the chaos and grabbed it as she continued on her journey reliving the craziness from the night before. “This just keeps getting better and better.” The whiskey she tossed at Mario’s head had splashed and more than likely stained the white and off white patterned wall paper. The plush carpet under her bare feet still felt damp from the water and mud Jacob tracked in with his boots.

“Jake—” A sob tore through her, temporarily cutting off the air to her lungs. She leaned against her bedroom door as a wave of nausea hit her. The angel in her dream told her Jacob was in the hospital fighting for his life. *Could it be true?* Could he really be on death’s door because of her selfishness? Julia fished through her purse for her phone and called the one person she knew would tell her the truth, whether she wanted to hear it or not.

“Julia? Are you okay? I’ve been calling your cell all morning.”

“I’ve really made a mess of things this time, Carm.”

“You can tell me all of it later. Right now, you need to get to the hospital. Jake was admitted last night.”

Julia sank to the floor. “So it’s true? He’s there fighting for his life because of me?” Fresh tears rolled down her cheeks.

“What do you mean because of you?”

"He walked in while I was screwing Mario here in the bed, he made for me."

Carmen gasped and remained silent for a moment. "Julia? Are you still there? Listen to me. Forget about that shit Mario for now. Pull yourself together and meet me here at the hospital. I have another meeting in an hour, but I'm free for a bit after that. I need to see you to be sure you're all right. I'll fill you in on Jake's condition then."

"I'm fine. Just give me a couple hours to get myself cleaned up and pulled together. I don't want you to see me like this. It's not pretty."

"I knew what I was getting into with you from day one, kitten. Nothing you can do or say is bad enough to make me abandon you and our friendship. When will you believe that?"

The hurt in her Carmen's voice cut Julia to her very core. She's right. She'd been by her side right from the beginning, even before her art started to take off. Could Carmen really be her soul mate? "It's taken me a long time, but I do believe you. I'll see you in a bit. Just please watch over Jake until I can get there to see him for myself."

"Julia, I don't think it's a good idea for you to try to see him right now. His family's with him. It's not the time or the place for a showdown with them, especially his brother. Jake's in ICU and only family are allowed access to him at this point."

"We'll just see about that." Julia tossed her phone onto the bed. The first item on her agenda for the day would be a hot shower to cleanse her body of the horror from the night before and then call the cleaning crew to work on the condo. Before the day was over, she hoped all remnants of her royal fuck up would be erased. Unfortunately, a man's life hung in the balance because of her actions. No amount of hot water and vanilla scented soap would make that disappear.

* * * *

Chapter 20

Carmen met Julia at the main entrance of the hospital and pulled her over to one of the more private waiting areas to explain what happened to Jacob the night before. "Dr. Evans is the best orthopedic surgeon we have, if not in the entire country. He's assembled an entire team of doctors and nurses to take care of Jake and ensure he has the best chance to survive. He's even more hopeful now since he made it through the last twelve hours. Besides the surgery scheduled for this afternoon to repair the fractures in his leg and arm, most of his care will be in the hands of the nurses. From this point on, we have to take it one day at a time. The doctors can repair his body, but his spirit is another thing altogether. That part's out of our hands."

"What do you mean? There's got to be more you can do for him. Bring in whoever Dr. Evans wants for his team and any equipment he needs. I don't care what it costs. Just make sure he makes it through this."

"Julia, it's not up to us. It's up to him. Jacob has to want to come back."

"Of course he wants to come back! He's got his whole life ahead of him. He can't just give up." Julia shivered and her arms covered with goose bumps as she recalled the conversation from her dream. Daniel told her Jacob needed to decide whether or not to stay on the Island or come back. Staying there would mean he would die here. Even though at the time, it sounded like the best option for herself, she'd be damned if she'd let it happen. "I have to tell him I'm sorry for what happened. Tell me where I have to go."

The Chief of Staff shook her head. "He hasn't been conscious at all since he was rushed in here last night. He won't be able to talk to you or let you know he can hear you."

"It doesn't matter if he can talk to me or not. I have to see him. I can't explain it, but I have to try, Carmen. I've never cared about who I hurt along the way to get what I wanted out of life. If it wasn't working for me, I got rid of it and that included people. I don't want to do that with Jake. He deserved more from me than what I gave him. Please tell me where I have to go in this place. I don't want to be wandering the halls up there with all the other patients and their families."

"You're not considered a part of his family and the Hartleys have every right to keep you out of the ICU. So far they've not asked to ban you from seeing Jake, but if you show up there today, it *will* happen. Please, just let me handle this. I'll keep you updated on his stay here hourly if that's what it takes."

"But I need to tell him he's got to fight to come back and be with his soul mate. If he stays away, he'll lose his chance and many other lives will hang in the balance."

"You're not making any sense. You pushed him away. Why would he want to come back? I think seeing you with another man would be enough to kill any love he felt for you."

"Not me. His soul mate is still out there, waiting for him. I know it sounds bizarre, but I believe it now. Just trust me on this. Even if it falls apart on me, I have to give it a try. I've run away from so many things and people in my life. It has to stop here—with Jake."

Carmen looked at her watch. "Damn. I have another appointment in fifteen minutes. There isn't any way you'd wait, so I could go with you to see him, is there?"

Julia shook her head. "I have to do this on my own. I'll check in with you afterward though. We have a lot to talk about too."

"Check in with the visitor's station behind us. They'll give you the pass you'll need to be able to have access to ICU." They stood and hugged each other before Carmen made her way back toward the elevators.

Julia on the other hand, walked down the corridor toward the gift shop. "Maybe if I come bearing gifts, the Hartleys won't toss me out on my ass."

* * * *

The sound of her high heels clicking in the hallway attacked her already frayed nerves like fingernails on a chalkboard. *Damn. I should have worn flats.* Julia rounded the corner and moved down the quiet hallway toward the room the ICU nurse told her she could find Jacob. Then she saw the one person she'd hoped to avoid. The look on his face nearly caused her to lose her footing. *Calm yourself down, Julia. You've come this far, there's no reason to chicken out now.*

Eric Hartley turned toward the noise of her heels and his jaw dropped open. "Speak of the devil herself." His stance told Julia that there was no way in hell he would let her near his brother's room.

She focused so keenly on not falling on her ass on the glossy floor that she didn't register Eric rapidly moving toward her. Before she knew it, he'd crossed the distance between them and roughly grabbed her arm. Too surprised to react otherwise, she didn't struggle at all, and allowed him to guide her into the open doorway of the family lounge. "Let go of me, Eric."

"Not a chance. Only family members are allowed to be up here and you definitely don't qualify." Eric kept his body between her and the doorway, blocking any view of Jacob's room.

Julia dropped the floral arrangement she carried on one of the tables in the lounge before whirling on Eric. "Like hell I don't. Jake and I have been together for two years. He proposed—"

"Cut the bullshit. I know all about your affair with Mario Carlos. Don't look so surprised. Kathy told me all about it and how she caught the two of you in the supply closet. I decided not to tell my mother or my sister that little bit of news. They've been through enough, hovering over him throughout the night. You have no right to be here, Julia. *You* are the reason he's in there fighting for his life and I'll be damned if you're going to give him another excuse to not come back."

Julia's eyes filled with tears and her body shook.

This appeared to surprise Eric enough that he loosened his grip on her arm.

"He's that bad? I tried to call but they wouldn't tell me anything or put me through to his room. I thought if I came here myself and apologized for hurting him, he'd listen and—"

"And what? He'd come out of his coma just because you decided to show up over twelve hours after he was nearly killed because of you? You're even more delusional than I gave you credit for."

Julia's mouth went dry. This definitely wasn't how she saw this going down. All she wanted to do was tell Jacob she was sorry and never meant to hurt him like this. She should have listened to Carmen, but once again she's fucked it all up. She wanted to tell Eric it'd been Carmen who told her about Jacob's condition, but thought better of it. If the Hartleys found out, Carmen's position at the hospital could be in jeopardy. "I've made a mess of everything, I know that. All I wanted was to find out how he was. No one would tell me more when I called to check on him."

"Of course not! No one is to get any updates but family. He's fighting for his life in there and I'll be damned if I'll let you anywhere near him while he does it. You want to make yourself useful? Instead of bringing flowers or any other gifts, how about you do us all a favor and pack up his things. I'll be by to pick them up in the next few days."

No matter how badly she felt about Jacob's accident, Julia wasn't about to let Eric or anyone else treat her like trash. "You can't order me around like some personal servant. You want his things? Come over and get them yourself. Make sure you bring plenty of boxes. Jake accumulated a lot of shit in the two years he's lived with me."

Eric rolled his eyes. "You really are a piece of work. First, you show up all weepy eyed and concerned, but all you really wanted to know is if he was still alive or not. I'm surprised you even showed your face around here."

"Why wouldn't I be here? The hospital should have called me first. I'm his emergency contact."

"They did. Don't you have someone to answer your phone for you? The hospital left no less than ten messages before they called my sister's house."

Julia wanted to smack the smug look off his face but kept still. "You're lying! No one called."

"Check. Your. Messages. Maybe you left the phone off the hook or forgot to turn your cell back on after you finished with one of your lovers?"

She'd heard enough and this time actually did try to slap him.

Eric caught her by the wrist. "Time to leave, Julia. You want to do this on your own or do I have to ask security to remove you from the building?"

Kathy poked her head into the lounge, her eyes wide. "Is there a problem?"

"What the fuck is she doing here?" Julia's face turned bright purple. "She's got no right to be near my Jake!"

Kathy appeared to grow three inches before Julia's eyes. "*Your* Jake? Funny. You seemed to have spread your legs for every man in town. What makes you think he's yours or that he even still wants to be with you after what you've done to him?"

Julia laughed. "Don't be so goody goody, Nurse Kathy. It's not my fault the honey between your thighs couldn't keep Mario satisfied." Now they'd done it. Julia went into bitch mode. This wasn't going to end up the way she'd hoped. In fact, it got worse by the minute. She needed to get out of there, but Eric still had her arm in a death grip cutting off her circulation as well as pissing her off. Enough was enough. They wanted to confront the mean and selfish Julia, now was their chance.

All color left Kathy's face. "Leave immediately or you will be physically removed and tossed out onto the street."

Pulling her arm free of Eric's grip, Julia squared her shoulders and walked toward Kathy. "Honey, the things we could've done together if you would've just played along."

"What the hell are you talking about?"

Julia reached out and touched Kathy's face with her fingertips, causing her to recoil.

Eric started toward them but stopped in his tracks.

The look Kathy gave him was enough to keep him back.

"All you had to do was keep quiet about Mario and me. You could've joined us for romps in the supply room. You can't tell me you haven't fantasized about it ever since you watched."

Eric stepped between the women, hiding Kathy from her view. "Get out, Julia. No one wants to hear any more of your twisted fantasies."

"Suit yourself." She sized him up and down. "Rumor has it you've already made a name for yourself working in the Vegas clubs. I'm beginning to wonder if I picked the wrong Hartley two years ago." She blew them both a kiss and sashayed down the deserted hallway, toward the elevators. She could feel their eyes on her as she made it down the long corridor. Her heels on the highly polished floor remained the only sound, and her heart beating wildly in her chest. *Keep walking. Don't look back. Don't you dare let them see you cry. Let them believe what they want to believe.* "Daniel? If you're really there, please stay with Jake and help him make the right choice."

* * * *

Her whispered heartfelt prayer didn't go unheard.

Jacob's father, Michael Hartley witnessed the whole thing. As Daniel's partner, he was in charge of watching over his son and several others. All of them were connected to his son and his soul mate Quinn Quartermarsh.

Although she couldn't see him, Michael knew she could feel his calming presence. He rested his hand on her arm and squeezed gently. Tears filled his angelic eyes as he escorted Julia toward the elevators. "Don't you worry about Jake now, darlin'. It's time you concentrated on your own healing. Go to Carmen and start your future together. We'll take care of the rest."

* * * *

Chapter 21

Julia didn't go home after the confrontation with Eric and Kathy. She did make it all the way down to the lobby and outside before halting. *Once again, I'm running away from my problems instead of working through them. I can't keep doing this.* Instead of heading to her car, she turned right back around and marched through the electronic sliding doors. She took the elevator up again, but this time two more floors above the Intensive Care Unit.

Holding her head high, she made her way to the receptionist who handled the entire floor. "I'm here to meet, Dr. Hall. I was hoping to talk to her before she headed out to the board meeting."

"Ms. Santos?" Julia smiled and nodded. "Go right on ahead. She's still in and asked me to keep my eye out for you if you came up this afternoon." The perky brunette smiled brightly and pointed toward the heavy oak doors that lead to Carmen's office.

Not that Julia needed the directions. She'd been in the office many times but never with her tail between her legs. She didn't relish having to relive the whole scene with Eric, but she promised she would tell her friend exactly what happened.

Julia broke down the minute she entered the room and witnessed the look on Carmen's face. *She told me this would happen and she has every right to say 'I told you so,' but that's not her way. I think I could take that now more than the sympathetic look in her eyes. Daniel's right. She's the only one who's never judged me, no matter how badly I've behaved.* It took Julia a moment to compose herself before she could fill Carmen in on what happened in the ICU. "I can't think of anything else right now. Jake's in this hospital fighting for his life and I'm sure by now, his family and doctors have banned me from getting anywhere near him. Can't you do something?"

Carmen brought Julia a glass of water and then leaned back against her desk. "I'm sorry. I can't change the rules of the hospital for anyone unless the family makes a special request. I tried to tell you that earlier, but for your sake I hoped I was wrong."

She looked into Carmen's icy blue eyes and knew it would do no good to plead her case any further.

"Besides darling, we have other things to worry about now. Mario is making some outrageous demands."

"So, what else is new? He's been full of himself right from the moment he finished his residency. It wasn't the wisest decision you ever made keeping him on staff here—and don't remind me that you only did it to keep me happy. Mario has delusions of grandeur. He thinks he can bark orders and people jump, very much like he runs the ER." She grabbed her handkerchief from her pocket book and dabbed at her tear streaked face.

"He does rule his department with an iron fist. I have to admit, he gets great results. Most of his staff respects him."

Julia snorted. "Not everyone feels that way. I don't think I'd call it respect, at all. It's fear. Mario is nothing more than a bully."

Carmen tilted her head, making her blonde curls fall over her forehead.

Julia wanted to reach out and brush them out of her eyes, but held back a moment, waiting for the words she knew would soon follow.

"I'm sure you're aware of his on again off again relationship with one of the night nurses."

Julia nodded and shrugged.

"Well, he was here in this office only a few hours ago, demanding Kathy Baker be fired."

"On what grounds? Did she do something to harm a patient? I mean, I just had an argument with her myself but you don't see me demanding she be fired. She's only trying to protect her patient—Jake." Julia knew exactly what Kathy did to get Mario's boxers in a bunch, but decided to hold that piece of information from Carmen just a little bit longer.

"He tried to create a case against her by making up some shit about her being insubordinate, slacking in her duties and trying to use their relationship to get special favors. You and I both know that's a lie."

Julia raised her eyebrows. "Oh? How so?"

Carmen chuckled. "As you said, the man is full of himself. It didn't take him long to brag to me that he was nailing you in the supply closet while Kathy watched. He said she was a threat to not only him, but to me. If I didn't fire her effective immediately, he was going to see to it that the Board found out about *our* relationship. He tried to act like he knew about it all along, but I could tell he was pissed."

Julia swallowed hard. This was exactly what she'd been afraid he'd try to pull. Even through Carmen told her repeatedly, her being a lesbian, she never wanted to be the reason the other hospital administrators turned against her. She didn't want Carmen to know she still worried about it, so she put on the tough girl act once again. "I tossed our affair out at Mario to get a rise out of him. He wouldn't take no for an answer and I wanted him out of my bed, out of my condo and out of my life. Finding out he wasn't the only one I'd been sleeping with for more than a few years got his attention. Finding out it was you, sent him over the edge. Of course, I conveniently left out one detail."

Carmen smiled. "We haven't been lovers for over two years."

Julia nodded. "If he wants to go to make a formal complaint about you, then let him. You've never made your sexual preferences a secret. Why would the Board give a shit about it now?"

"I'm not concerned about me. You have a reputation to consider too. You made it clear to your adoring public you were with Jake. Now if all of this comes out—"

"All it would do is to create more buzz about my gallery. I love sex, Carmen, with men *and* women. I use it as an escape and a weapon. It's all I think about even when my life is a complete mess. You've known that right from the day we met. No man has been in my life as long as you have."

Carmen got up from her desk and joined Julia on the love seat, taking her hand. "I know and you mean the world to me. I just don't want anything to hurt you." She squeezed her hand a bit and brought it to her lips. "And don't go pulling the tough chick act with me. I know you're worried about my reputation here. It just makes me love you all the more."

Julia leaned over and kissed Carmen softly at first, touching her honey-hued skin, then deepening the kiss as she felt Carmen relax in her arms. She loved the feel of this woman and all of her curves. It's what attracted Julia to her in the first place, those classic Botticelli hips and thighs. She couldn't get enough of her when they were together. It'd been far too long, and Carmen had been so patient. Julia knew it was wrong to let her lust for her friend bubble up now, but she couldn't help it. She needed the comfort and guidance only Carmen could give to her.

Carmen abruptly broke their kiss, panting. "I'm due at a hospital meeting in twenty minutes. How about you go home, and pick up the overnight bag you always have packed. Get out of that condo for a few days and let me work out your stresses for you."

Julia felt the sudden rush of hot fluid between her thighs and she actually blushed. The last time Carmen worked out her kinks, she found herself on the receiving end of a humongous dildo. Carmen feasted on every inch of her, worked her with the paddle and then tied her to the bed while fucking her with the strap on. Both women had been in heaven in their roles as Domme and sub. No one ever gave Julia as much pleasure or cared for her more.

Jacob cared for her but it wasn't the same. Carmen was the only one who could give her what her heart, body and soul craved—the ability to completely surrender and be dominated by her lover. *To hell with what anyone thinks. They already see me as a selfish cunt. Why not just give in to what I've been searching for all along?*

"I would love to spend the next week with you. You always know exactly what I need." She kissed Carmen again, running her fingers through her curly, pale blonde hair, chasing her tongue slowly, giving her just a taste of her submission. If they had more time, Julia would submit completely, right there in her office.

Carmen smiled and helped her from the couch. "Go ahead and make yourself at home. I'll be there just after six. Make sure to wear the thigh high boots and the bells."

Julia shivered and bit her lip, lowering her eyes. "I'll be strapped in and waiting for your instructions, Mistress."

* * * *

Chapter 22

Eric ended up being right. The hospital *did* call numerous times. Unfortunately, all the messages were directed to the gallery number. Julia spent all of her free time there, so it just seemed much easier to have Darla handle everything. With all that happened last night, Julia completely forgot to stop the calls from being forwarded to her assistant. Once again, thanks to Mario's inability to keep his dick in his pants, Darla no longer remained in her employ and Julia would need to scramble to find another who could handle the workload.

Luckily, Amber seemed ripe for the picking.

Having hired her just before the opening to help Darla keep things running smoothly, Amber should be more than familiar with what Julia expected of an assistant. She also seemed thankful for the opportunity to prove she could handle it as well as Darla did. If she wasn't so pressed to get over to Carmen's, she would've loved to explore just how grateful the perky strawberry blonde UCLA co-ed could be. Maybe Carmen would like to invite Amber into their future play dates? Julia's nipples hardened at the thought of being completely submissive to two dommes at once—definitely one more thing she wanted to add to her sexual bucket list.

After making sure Amber was settled in at the gallery, her cell phone charged and no longer transferring calls, Julia headed to the condo to pick up her overnight bag. She already had a large wardrobe at Carmen's spacious home. It was filled with all of her favorite pieces, some of which Carmen purchased for her. So it wasn't necessary for Julia to take any of her clothes or lingerie she'd need at the condo. Besides, if her Mistress had her way, and Julia knew she would, she'd be clothed in very little if at all, for the entire week. Thigh high patent leather boots, bells clamped to her nipples and pussy lips would be the norm and her body hummed at the thought of it.

The crew of housekeepers Julia hired did a wonderful job cleaning up the condo after the bloody mess Mario left of the place. No traces of blood or dirt were on the white carpet or rugs. The table top once covered in candle wax now shined with fresh polish. Brand new candles adorned the silver holders. Not a trace of the chaos from the night before remained, but the sterility of the whole scene reminded her of the hospital. As she breezed through the open doorway to her bedroom, she was struck by how lonely and empty the room appeared. Her heart clenched and the tears formed in her eyes, looking at the beautiful bed Jacob built for her.

Glaring at her reflection in the mirrored closet doors, she screamed in frustration. "Why couldn't I be satisfied with just him? He didn't deserve to be hurt this way and yet I still did it, keeping him for myself while knowing all along I would push him away." Her own voice sounded foreign to her. She'd never felt so sad or let anyone see this side of her. No one, except Carmen.

Julia ran her fingers over the filmy curtains surrounding the bed and sighed— just one more thing to be taken away before she could go on with her life. She needed to ask Amber to take care of it while she was away. She couldn't bear to watch it taken apart.

The boxes filled with Jacob's things sat on the floor, neatly labeled and sealed tight, ready to ship. It was yet another perk to having the housekeeping service. Julia could avoid touching all of his things, smelling his scent of him on his clothes, and torturing herself any more than she already did since the moment he walked in on her and Mario. The boxes were actually ready in time for the confrontation with Eric, but she would be damned if she would give him the satisfaction of knowing she'd already packed up Jacob's belongings.

It seemed better this way and Julia knew it deep down in her soul. It would've been only a matter of time before she hurt him anyway, but she wished he wasn't fighting for his life now because of her. Broken hearts can always mend, but multiple broken bones and a broken spirit may not. She closed her eyes and wished Jacob made the right choice to come back from the Island. If a god or goddess did watch over everyone, she prayed they worked their magic for him. "I know I have no right to ask for anything for me. But please, if you're out there, watch over him. Help him find his true soul mate and forget about me." She opened her eyes to find she wasn't alone.

"He's found her, Julia. Now it's time to get you to yours." A woman with long curly auburn hair spoke to her. She wore a flowing dark emerald gown, matching her eyes. Julia never saw anyone more beautiful in her life or in her dreams.

Daniel smiled and quickly made the introductions. "Julia, this is Lady Fate. She's one of The Three and in charge of your Destiny."

Julia looked between the two, trying to find her voice. "I—I thought I dreamt about you. You're real?"

The Goddess's laughter tickled her ears and brought an immediate smile to Julia's face. She'd never felt more at ease with anyone, even while feeling terrified she might be losing her marbles.

"You're most definitely not dreaming now, nor are you losing your sanity, child. Daniel *is* your Guardian Angel. He thought it was time to give you a little extra push to get you to see the right path."

Julia hung her head and knew her cheeks burned crimson. "I don't deserve this second chance. I'm the reason Jake's fighting for his life."

"No. You're not the reason he's there. It's true your actions helped set certain things in motion. It's time to stop blaming yourself and accept you cannot change what's happened up until this point in this lifetime for yourself or for Jacob. You played a role in helping get him to where he needs to be with his heart and soul, and now it's your turn. The one you've been bonded to through each and every life awaits you. You've stayed away from her long enough. The two of you have always been destined to be together and now it's up to you."

Julia shook her head as fresh tears rolled down her cheeks. "I'm afraid to give my heart to anyone and most of all I'm afraid I'll destroy Carmen, like I nearly destroyed Jake, like—"

"How your parents nearly destroyed you?" Daniel's voice softly whispered her worst fear and deepest, darkest secret.

She swallowed the lump in her throat but couldn't speak.

He reached for both of her trembling hands, squeezing them. "They took away your innocence and childhood but they could *never* break your spirit. You did what you had to do to survive. Yes, you've been a selfish bitch, but you created the tough persona to get through each day. You buried the past long enough. Now it's time you start facing all that pain, so you can really put it behind you."

Fate smiled and nodded. "You must choose. The life of Julia Santos as the selfish, lonely, made up celebrity persona or Julia Santos the beautiful, loving creature who will get to experience the love of one who will cherish her heart and soul forever?"

Julia was stunned. "I have a choice? I mean, it's not too late?"

Both Daniel and Fate nodded and continued to wait for her response to their question.

Julia fell to her knees and placed her hands over her heart. "I choose Carmen. I choose the path that leads me to our life together, even though I must relive the nightmares I've buried long ago. I choose Carmen."

The Goddess smiled brightly. "Very well. We will leave you now to begin your journey. Remember, we're watching and will help you get through it all, every step of the way."

"Go on. Carmen's waiting." Daniel winked.

Julia watched them fade away. Even though she was now alone in the room, she wasn't afraid any longer. She knew what she needed to do. Julia rolled her shoulders and wiped the tears from her eyes one last time.

Her phone chirped with a message from Amber asking if there might be anything else she needed from her for the day.

She looked around the room and nodded then typed out her text. "There are several boxes in my bedroom. Please have them sent to the address on file for Maredyth Cooke. She'll know what they are and what to do with them." She paused for a moment, nearly second guessing her decision. "See to it that the bed in the master bedroom is dismantled and found a good home. Sell it or donate it to charity. I'll leave it up to you to figure out the details."

Carmen will make sure I'm punished for what I've done, and help me work through it all. Julia felt safe and secure under Carmen's care. Lady Fate and Daniel were right. It was time she admitted to herself who held her heart all along. It'd always been Carmen she needed as her Domme. Trying to mold Jacob into her only made Julia long for more and keep searching for it in so many others. Jacob was a willing partner and lover, but he truly wasn't a Dom, at least not one who could control her. Julia felt safe with him yes, but it just wasn't the same. She needed so much more than Jacob could possibly give her, and it was wrong of her to try to force him into that role.

Knowing he was in good hands on the Island with his soul mate, helped her see in order for her to move forward, she had to go back. She had to give herself over completely to Carmen's care. She needed the discipline and safety only her Mistress could give her.

Her pulse raced and her palms became sweaty by the time she pulled her Mustang out of its parking space in the garage. The realization hit her like a ton of bricks. Carmen had always been the Top to her Bottom. Julia enjoyed being a Top from time to time, but her true self was that of Carmen's sub. She shook her head in wonder. The visit to the Island and now actually speaking to the Goddess herself helped to finally make up her mind. Butterflies fluttered in her stomach while she felt an excitement she'd only experienced with Carmen. This could be the journey she craved her whole life, and it'd been right in front of her the entire time. *Was this what it felt like to finally realize you've found your soul mate?*

* * * *

Chapter 23

February 12th, Present Day Las Vegas

Julia was surprised by how much she enjoyed her dinner with Jacob and Quinn. Once they got through the initial awkwardness of seeing each other again, he not only heard her out but told her the words she only dreamed she'd hear from him one day.

Jacob forgave her.

Carmen was right all along. The only person holding up her recovery from her past was Julia herself. Sitting at the table, with tears in her eyes and nearly breathless from laughter, she wished once again, Carmen could see her now.

Jacob continued with his story, oblivious to anyone else in the restaurant besides the three of them. His face positively glowed as he talked about his children. "I've watched Quinn handle the little monsters during diaper changes like a pro, so I thought it was high time I gave it a try myself. I mean how much trouble could the two of them be?"

Quinn nearly choked on the water she sipped. "Picture it. There he is frantically searching for another diaper while at the same time, little Daniel discovers the ability to pee straight up in the air and hit his Daddy in the eye!"

Julia wiped the tears from her eyes and shook her head. "Oh my god, Jake! Everyone knows you have to keep a spare in hand for a little boy when changing diapers. As soon as the air hits their naked bottom half, they turn into Old Faithful."

"It gets even better. Stephanie wasn't about to be outdone by her brother." Quinn giggled a bit more before continuing, "She grabbed the bottle of powder and shook it like mad, covering all three of them in a blizzard of fine corn starch."

Jacob chuckled. "There we were covered in powder and Danny shot more pee in the air. Both of them looked at me and I swear they were going to start bawling and wake up Quinn, but no. Not *my* children. They giggled and cheered. The more I shook the powder out of my hair, the harder they laughed. It wasn't my finest hour as a parent, but I have to tell you, it was the most memorable. Of course it wasn't until the next day Quinn admitted she'd witnessed the whole thing."

"Well, I had to let you fly solo sometime and the three of you were laughing and enjoying yourselves way too much for me to interfere. It wasn't easy keeping hidden from the twins, but turning their daddy into a urine soaked snowman kept them distracted long enough for me to head back to bed."

Julia could barely breathe through her laughter, picturing the sight of Jacob and his giggling children. She held up her hand, hoping to get a few moments to compose herself.

Her laughter only seemed to spurn him on. "Oh, you think that's bad? Let me tell you what happened when I tried to clean them up!" Quinn lost it then and so did a few other diners near them. Out of the corner of her eye, Julia noticed a man making his way toward their table from the bar. "From the look of things, I'd say your dinner meeting is a success." Steve's emerald eyes appeared to dance in the candle light. "Mind if I join you?"

Damn. I know I've seen those eyes before. Of course! Lady Fate has the same eyes. I can't believe I didn't place it when we first met. This trip is just filled with surprises. Julia could only manage to nod through her laughter and motioned for him to take a seat next to her. "They've been telling me a bit of what it's like to raise twin toddlers. For the life of me, I don't know how they do it. I'm exhausted just hearing the stories. But this last one with the picture of Jake standing there covered in baby powder and getting shot in the eye with pee was just too much. I swear I nearly pissed myself right here in your restaurant."

Steve smiled broadly. "That's one of my favorite stories too. I wish you guys had the nanny cam set up then. The video of that night would be priceless!" He signaled to the bartender to send his drink over to the table before he continued. "Steph and Danny are a handful; I'll grant you that, but also a joy. From the moment I first held them in my arms in the delivery room, I've been head over heels in love."

Surprised yet again, Julia simply stared at Steve for a moment. "Wait? You were there when they were born?" *This just keeps getting better and better.*

Jacob answered for him, "Just about the entire family was there. The twins didn't want to be left out of the party and demanded to come into the world on our wedding day."

"They were kicking up a storm all day long, but at least they waited until the reception to decide they wanted out. I was dancing when my water broke. Unbeknownst to me, Jake and Steve had a plan in place in case something happened. Before I knew it, we were at the hospital and I was swearing up a storm."

Steve laughed outright. "You started up with the swearing as soon as Nathan picked you up and headed for the exit." He glanced at Julia before taking a gulp of his drink. "Nathan is a friend and the owner of a private security company and limo service. I trust him with my life and of those in my inner circle whenever I travel to California. In fact, now that you've agreed to work for me, his car service will be at your beck and call. He has offices in LA too."

Julia smiled. "I just may take you up on that when having to face the nasty traffic going to and from LAX."

"You'll get to meet him if you plan on staying here for a few more days. He's flying in for our anniversary party and of course to see the twins. He's another one who spoils the hell out of them." Quinn reached across the table and squeezed Julia's hand tightly. "Please say both you and Carmen will come."

"I'm...are you sure?" Julia stuttered a bit, unsure what to say. She knew what Carmen's answer would be. She'd want to try anything to push the boundaries a bit. To have Julia face all her demons and attend a party where Jacob's family were all going to be in attendance would do just that.

Jacob nodded. "I can't think of a better way to celebrate how both of us have moved on and found our soul mates. Besides, you got to meet Quinn. I'd like to see Carmen again. The memories I have of her are pretty sketchy. She visited me when I was in the coma. I couldn't answer her, but I knew she was there."

Steve bumped her upper arm with his shoulder. "Come on Ms. Santos. Where's your spirit of adventure? You won over Eric. Now you get a chance to win over Katrina Hartley."

Julia giggled and nodded. "I've actually written to her a few times over the last year, but chickened out at the last minute, never mailing the first letters. Last week, after Carmen told me she sent her letter to you, I sent mine to your mother. Her response to me was a Vegas post card with just three words."

Steve leaned into her again and wiggled his eyebrows. "Don't leave us hanging here. What did she write on that card?"

"See you soon."

Her three companions erupted in laughter.

"So, I can take that as a good thing?"

Jacob smiled broadly. "Oh yeah. I've been wondering why she's been so interested in whether or not I agreed to see you tonight. I have a feeling if either one of us tried to chicken out, we'd never hear the end of it and she'd make damn sure we were in the same room with each other before she flew back home to Indiana."

Julia placed her elbows on the table and rested her head in her hands. "Okay, let's get back to the story about the babies interrupting your wedding reception. How is it again that Steve ended up in the delivery room with you two?"

Steve's bawdy laughter rang out in the restaurant, causing a few other diners to grin in response. "If you heard the obscenities flying out of Quinn's mouth that night, you would've come out for reinforcements too. I tried to beg off but Jake was persistent."

"Yeah, I begged you not to let me go back in there with her like that. I needed him there to distract her. She delivered them naturally. Danny and Steph weren't going to wait for the doctors to prep their mother for surgery."

Julia shook her head in amazement. "Wow! You two really have had a crazy life together after the Island."

"Oh, is that what you've been talking about tonight?"

"It's an amazing story. Imagine being able to meet your soul mate thirteen years before you actually lay eyes on each other here in Vegas. Have you two been able to go back since then?"

"There's one more visit we didn't tell you about yet." Jacob's eyes clouded over and he reached for Quinn's hand.

To Julia, it looked like he was clutching it for dear life.

She looked between the three of them and waited for someone to answer. "What? You look like you've seen a ghost, Jake."

Steve spoke up first, "We nearly lost both of them on that Island two years ago."

"I don't understand. I thought it was all settled. Didn't you help them get together finally?

Steve smiled and shrugged his shoulders.

Quinn spoke softly, still overcome by emotion after all this time. "That he did. He stuck by me after I had a nervous breakdown—"

"Because of me." Jacob's voice cracked and he looked to his friend as if wanting him to help explain...

Steve took another gulp of his scotch. "These two were separated by circumstances a little out of their control. I admit, back then I wanted to have Quinn all for myself, but I knew the only one who'd truly make her happy was Jake. She was the only one who could do the same for him. So, instead of waiting for them to figure it out, I took matters into my own hands."

"I'm still lost." Julia searched Quinn's face for answers. "When did you have a nervous breakdown?"

"About two months after I found out Jake was going to marry someone else."

"What?" Julia sat back heavily against her chair. She knew she couldn't hide the shock showing on her face. *It's my fault. I nearly cost him his chance to be with this beautiful woman. Goddess, forgive me.*

Jacob nodded. "Yep. It wasn't the smartest move on my part, but I thought she'd be better off with Steve. He could give her everything I couldn't."

"Except her heart belonged to you and always did." Steve gazed over at Julia. "I took care of her the best I could and then told Jake to straighten up and fly right or I'd fight tooth and nail to keep her for myself."

"Holy Shit! I think I need another drink, maybe a double."

Quinn laughed. "I told you our story is full of twists."

"You weren't kidding. How did you nearly lose both of them on the Island?" She turned in her seat to face Steve, her eyes wide, pleading with him to continue.

"This part is still a bit of a mystery to all of us, but it seems both traveled back to the Island in their dreams, searching for the other. Once they were there—"

"I didn't want to go back. There was too much pain and I didn't want to live without her. Once I had her in my arms there in paradise, I never wanted to let her go. I begged her to stay there with me forever."

Julia's spine tingled as goose bumps instantly covered her body. "But you couldn't do that. People here needed you in their lives."

Jacob stared at her for a few beats and knit his eyebrows together. "Exactly. As much pain as we were in we couldn't put it off on those we loved. Instead, we spent every moment they allowed us to have together before we had to come back and fight for what was ours. How did you know that?"

Her eyes filled with tears once again. "It seems we have a lot more in common than I first realized. I made it to the Island too. After the fight with you and then with Mario, I just wanted to sleep for a bit. I'd made such a mess with things and I couldn't face it any more. I took a few of the pain pills left from my last stay in the hospital, hoping to drop off into a dreamless sleep for a few hours. Unfortunately, I didn't take into account all the whiskey I had in my system."

"So like me, you were there because you were between life and death?" Jacob's blue eyes bored into hers. "You didn't try to kill yourself did you?"

"No, but once I was there, even before I found out why, I'd already made up my mind I wasn't going to go back."

Steve cleared his throat and put his arm around her.

She didn't realize she'd been trembling until she felt his reassuring hug.

"Who convinced you to change your mind?"

Julia smiled. "I can't get anything by you, now can I?"

Steve shook his head.

Julia looked directly at Quinn. "Some beautiful young hunk covered in tattoos and piercings told me I couldn't stay. He told me you were there with Jake, sealing your fated bond with each other and that I had way too much living to do...with Carmen."

Quinn reached for Julia's hands across the table. "You met my brother Danny?"

She nodded. "That's a story for another night if you don't mind. It took me a few days to believe it all actually happened and I've never told Carmen the entire story. I'd like to tell you everything when she's with us, so she can hear it all too."

"It's a date." Quinn squeezed Julia's hands one more time before letting go. "It makes me very proud to know my little brother has indeed found his calling as a Guardian Angel."

Julia wiped the last of the tears from her eyes and smiled. "You should be proud of him. He's definitely not who I'd expect to see standing in front of me, introducing themselves as my Guardian. Hell, I didn't think someone like me deserved to have one."

"If The Three feel we're worthy, who are we to say otherwise." Steve's deep voice was barely a whisper over the din of the other restaurant patrons, but Julia heard him clearly.

"That's exactly what Danny told me on more than one occasion over the years. Are you sure you don't have something you want to share with us tonight too, Steve?" Julia leaned in closer to the Vegas tycoon and raised her eyebrows up and down, much like he did to her earlier.

He chuckled. "That as you say, is a story for another time. How about you tell us a bit more about how you finally figured out Carmen was your one and only?"

Quinn laughed. "Don't mind him, Julia. Steve is the master at deflecting attention from him and onto others. We'll get him to spill his story at some point. I may have to break out the big guns though."

"You wouldn't." Steve's slow grin seemed to be infectious to everyone at the table.

"What're the big guns?" Julia didn't know what she was smiling about, but she couldn't help herself.

Jacob laughed at Steve's fake misery. "Quinn's sister makes the best damn cinnamon rolls I've ever tasted. Steve is a sucker for them and even flies back to Michigan when he's in need of a fix. Quinn's 'threatening' to have Miranda whip up a batch and torture him with the ooey gooey confections until he cracks. It's been our experience that he can't last more than five minutes after the rich vanilla and cinnamon aromas hit his nose."

"Not so. I did last to seven minutes...once."

"Only because Miranda's three boys were holding you down!"

Steve signaled to the waiter for another round. "We'll just see about that when the time comes. If memory serves me, Julia was just about to tell us a bit more about her love story with Carmen."

Quinn was right. Steve Eischer seemed to definitely be a man of mystery when he wanted to be and very skilled at turning the spotlight onto others.

She sensed he might be a kindred spirit from the moment they met, so it wasn't any surprise to her when she began to tell her dinner companions all about the night she finally surrendered to what her heart knew all along.

* * * *

Chapter 24

Thirteen Years Ago, Los Angeles

"I've had just about enough of your nonsense, Mario. If you don't stop this crusade to have Kathy fired, you'll find yourself without a job. Having your own complaints about her is one thing, but trying to coerce other doctors into trashing her reputation is simply beyond unethical. I won't let you drag this hospital through the muck, just so you can exert your power over another one of your nurses."

"What the hell are you referring to? *Another* one of my nurses?" Mario continued to stare at her while wearing his usual smug look as if he didn't have a clue as to what she was talking about and really couldn't care less.

He honestly thought he could play stupid with her and Carmen wasn't going to put up with it. Even though he looked like hell with the broken jaw and the black eyes, she harbored absolutely no sympathy for him. As far as she was concerned, Mario was lucky a broken jaw was all he got from Jacob. While she missed the intimacy they once shared, Carmen never once forced the issue with Julia after Jacob entered the picture. The same couldn't be said about Mario.

Not only did he pursue Julia relentlessly, he'd managed to manipulate her into thinking she controlled their affair. Now he had the nerve to sit across from her and play the victim. "You know damn well what I'm talking about. You don't have any grounds to fire Kathy. Every other doctor in the ER and the other departments give her high marks for her work ethic and patient care. You can't make up shit and expect it to stick when there's overwhelming evidence to the contrary." Carmen let that sink in a moment before she continued, "There isn't anything that goes on in your department that I'm not privy to, so why don't we just cut the bullshit."

"I'm not going to sit here and be told I can't hire or fire whoever I want in my department. I run a tight ship in the ER. Anyone who can't cut it is out, plain and simple. You knew that when you put me in charge." He kept his teeth clenched as he spoke giving him an even more threatening expression than what was normal for him.

Carmen reached into the top drawer of her desk for a stack of files. Spreading them out in front of them on her desk, she gave him one more opportunity to figure it out on his own.

He shrugged and looked back to her for an explanation.

"Really? You don't remember any of these names? Each and every single one is a nurse or doctor who transferred out of your department within the last five years. All of them came to me, complaining about you and your sexually inappropriate behavior. They asked for transfers to get away from you and your threats to have them fired if they didn't keep sleeping with you."

Mario ran his hands over the files and snorted. "Oh please. All of them pursued me. I just gave them what they wanted. Some actually begged me to fuck them."

"That may very well be the case with a few of them, but when they wanted to break things off, you were the one to threaten their job security. In the eyes of the law, that's sexual harassment any way you cut it. This seems to be a pattern for you." Carmen fanned out the files even farther before going on, "Lucky for you, they were all willing to wait while we investigated. The evidence is pretty convincing, especially since every one of them have similar stories. You've opened this hospital up for multiple lawsuits and now you want to have your girlfriend fired because she caught you fucking one of your patients. You're supposed to be a leader in this hospital. Your behavior's disgusting."

Mario snorted. "You're just doing this to get rid of me because of my relationship with Julia." Even with his eyes swollen and bruised, he still pulled off a condescending eye roll.

Carmen bit her tongue and held her breath in order to keep herself from laughing in his face.

"I'm just giving her some space to get through this with Hartley and then we can get married." He waved his hand in front of his face as if to dismiss her.

She couldn't believe the audacity of the man before her. Is he so self-absorbed that he *couldn't* see the writing on the wall? "I've known about you from day one. There isn't anything that went on between the two of you that she didn't share with me. You claim to be in love with her and yet you don't listen to a damn word she said. Julia planned to give you the boot and last night in the condo was to be your last, whether Jacob walked in on you or not."

Mario laughed. "You believe what you want. I know for a fact, Julia loved me and wanted the life I could give her. She just needed time to cut Hartley loose. Now that he's out of the picture, we can finally be open with our relationship. Oh, and don't think I'm going to tolerate her carrying on with you anymore. Those days are over."

Carmen smiled broadly. He must have some sort of concussion. No one really could be this oblivious to the consequences of their own actions. He lived in complete and utter denial of what happened the night before. The proof all but spelled out in front of him, but Mario simply refused to see it. She almost felt sorry for him. *Almost.* "You're one self-centered bastard. Do you really think she'd be saddled with the man who reminds her every single day of how she pushed Jacob over the edge and into our ICU, fighting for his life?"

"What the hell are you talking about now? Hartley isn't here. I would've been told."

"Given your present condition, it's understandable you'd be out of the loop around here."

"Carmen, you're not making any sense. Why don't you stop talking in circles and just give it to me straight. I've been here since I left Julia's last night and have yet to get any sleep. I had to have my jaw wired shut because of that hot head, and was released from the orthopedics ward just before you summoned me to your office. I haven't had time to check in, but someone on the staff would've informed me if he ended up in my emergency room."

"If you were still on staff at this hospital, you might still be privy to that information."

He stared at her as the color drained from his face.

For a moment, Carmen thought he was going to pass out, but instead he crossed his arms over his chest and sat straight up in his chair. "Are you firing me?"

"If it comes down to it, I *will* present these files to the board and they *will* support me on it. I would prefer you resign."

"On what grounds?" Mario continued to appear calm and collected.

She wondered again if he could really be this clueless or if it was just an act. "Seriously? Have you not heard one word I've said to you since you sat down in that chair?" Carmen tossed her pen down on top of the files and stared at him. "Do you really think this hospital's going to be dragged through all the bad publicity of one sexual harassment lawsuit let alone ten? If you care about your future as a doctor at all, you will resign—"

"And if I don't?" Mario sat back and crossed his legs.

"If you don't, I'll see to it the California Medical Board is informed of your other 'relationships' with your patients." Carmen pulled more files from her desk and tossed them on top of the others already fanned out before them. "You really get around, Mario."

"You've no proof of any of that."

Even as he voiced those words, Carmen saw some of his macho resolve fade away and be replaced with something she never thought she'd see from this man—a little bit of fear. She had him dead to rights and admittedly she felt great pleasure watching him squirm just a bit. She kept one last ace up her sleeve. She hoped it wouldn't have to come down to using it, but the doctor left her no choice.

"Did you forget about the cameras in all the supply closets? Not only do I have footage of you with Julia, but also of at least six other patients who just so happen to make repeat visits to *your* ER. No one is that accident prone, and definitely not this many women. All of them have been under your care with each visit."

"You can't do this. We're all consenting adults. No one was forced to do anything, so there's no crime other than poor judgment of choosing where to get our freak on."

"I wouldn't be so sure of that, Mario. There's also footage of you giving a few of them pills. It won't take much to convince the Medical Board about how these women were having sex with you for drugs." Carmen opened another file and pushed a single page toward him. "Now, sign this letter of resignation and I'll make sure you get your glowing recommendation for any hospital you want to go to, as long as it's not in Los Angeles."

Mario snatched the pen she offered and scrawled his signature over the bottom then shoved the paper back across the desk. "I know you've had it in for me from day one. What is it? Can't stand the competition?"

"You're forgetting one thing here. I was the one who hired you to run *my* ER. Your abilities as a doctor were never and have never been in question. It's your inability to keep your dick in your pants that got you here today with only a few bruises and a broken jaw. I'm trying to give you a dignified way out, whether you believe it or not."

"Why? I would think you'd be thrilled to have me humiliated in front of everyone in this hospital and this city. Why do you give a shit?"

"Humiliating you in public would serve no purpose other than raining bad press down on the hospital. As much as I would love to watch you try to talk your way out of this, my first priority is the care of our patients." She leaned back in her chair and sighed. "On a more personal level, I believed you when you said you were in love with Julia. I'm counting on you to take the high road and let her go. You're not what she needs in her life now. She needs time to figure it all out for herself, without any more distractions. I can't choose her path for her, but I can make that path a little less cluttered."

"Good God! You're in love with her too."

Carmen nodded. "I have been since the moment I laid eyes on her. The difference between you and me is that I've let her go to find out what she wanted. You know the old saying about loving someone enough to set them free?"

"That's for hopeless romantics like Kathy. You stick to that idea of a happily ever after and you'll always be alone. If you want something or someone in this world, you've got to go out and get it and never let go. Maybe if you kept Julia happy in your bed, she wouldn't have gone looking for love all over town. I give her what she needs."

"Good luck with that. If Julia loves you like you think she does, she'll come back to you when she's ready and not a moment before."

Mario shook his head. "When she comes to her senses and realizes she wants me back in her life, she's going to have to do some serious groveling."

Carmen sighed. Before her was a man who would never be happy with himself or anyone in his life. He'll always be looking for the bigger and better thing and miss the happiness that could be his if he just opened his eyes. Now she really did feel sorry for him. He would be one lonely man. His delusions as to what he meant to Julia were the saddest part of all to her.

She'd met some real shits who claimed to be Doms and here sat another one right in front of her. He would never change and it really wasn't up to her to convince him to try. Now that he no longer worked at the hospital, she didn't have to care about him one way or another but she wasn't about to let him leave her office without one more dig. "That's the difference between you and me, Dr. Carlos. I truly love Julia, warts and all. I've let her go, so she can fly. If we *are* meant to be, she'll come back to me and it will be her *choice*.

* * * *

Chapter 25

Thirteen years ago, Long Beach, California

The hot bath laced with jasmine oil helped her relax. Julia hadn't realized just how tense her entire body was until she was completely submerged in the large sunken spa tub in Carmen's master bathroom. She'd forgotten how much she enjoyed just soaking in this tub. It'd been far too long since she stayed here. Julia became determined to change that.

During the drive out of the city toward Long Beach, she knew she finally moved in the right direction in her life for once. All these years, she put her passion into her art and the various muses along the way. Now, she headed toward her heart's desire. The one person who accepted her for who she was from the start—someone strong enough to take her in hand when she needed it and who'd been right by her side all along. Julia hoped it wasn't too late to give herself over to her Mistress completely.

She stepped out of the tub and reached for one of the large fluffy towels to dry off her now relaxed body. Her hair sat piled on top of her head, clamped in one of the banana clips she found in the vanity drawer. It looked like it'd been hand crafted by using two pieces of jade and it made Julia smile. It was the very first gift she'd given to Carmen after their trip to Hawaii almost

13 years ago. The color looked beautiful in her blonde hair and actually made several appearances in Julia's paintings. She always respected Carmen's wishes to not put her into any of her artwork, but seeing the jade hair clip always made both of them smile and reminisce.

Looking back at her reflection in the mirror she saw the shy gray-eyed little girl who first came to LA, hoping to make it big and prove everyone from her home town in Missouri wrong. She wasn't a freak or trailer trash like her parents. She was *somebody* and it was time to reclaim her true self. Julia left the bathroom and walked naked toward the large walk-in closet. She went directly to the chest of drawers on the far corner and opened the top drawer. Inside, she found the boxes of bell clamps Mistress directed her to wear. After choosing one of the boxes, she then turned to peruse the rest of the closet.

She didn't have far to look for the boots. A shelf of several pairs sat to her left. One pair in particular, spoke to her. Without hesitation, she chose the patent leathers with the five inch heels that laced from the top to toe. Of course there was a zipper on the inside of the boot to make it easier to get them on and off, but Julia never felt sexier than when she slowly laced herself up in those boots.

The clamps were coated with latex to help them grip to her flesh comfortably and yet hold on tight enough to not slip off during play sessions. The weight of the bells caused the clamps to tug on her nipples each time her breasts moved. Nothing like that sensation ever existed for Julia before and she felt the immediate rush of warmth between her thighs with each jiggle and jingle of her tits. To attach the last two clamps, she needed to sit on the bed and spread her legs wide. Grasping first her right and then her left outer pussy fold between her thumb and forefinger, she fit the clamps into place. There was a separate ring on each of the clamps where Mistress could attach a fine gold chain leash, tugging on it to keep Julia's attention focused on the tasks at hand, and reminding her not to cum until given permission.

* * * *

Carmen presented most of her findings concerning Dr. Carlos to the hospital Board of Directors. The fact he 'voluntarily' resigned made all of them happy to avoid a long drawn out fight. It seemed as far as they were concerned, that part of his case was closed. Carmen felt relieved as well. She didn't look forward to have to present all of the evidence gathered against Mario. The board members didn't need to know all the sordid details about the patients he slept with, and Carmen felt confident those women would keep quiet to protect their own reputations.

Now came the tricky part, what to do about the ten employees who seemed to have legitimate complaints, concerning sexual harassment. After nearly an hour of heated debate, they finally agreed to settle out of court if any of the women changed their mind and decided to file a formal complaint.

Carmen already knew from her previous discussions that all of them would be satisfied to know Mario would no longer be on staff and wouldn't be able to harass them again. Each of them already turned in notarized letters, requesting he be transferred to another department or be fired from the hospital altogether, as the only stipulation to avoid a lawsuit.

Once the board meeting adjourned at nearly 5:45pm, Carmen thought she would be exhausted, but instead she felt strangely revitalized. Not only did she appease the Board, she'd been able to lend her support to hard working nurses and doctors who were being treated like sex toys, instead of the award winning professionals they were.

Walking through the ER on her way out of the building, Carmen immediately sensed the change in the air. The place seemed to be as busy as ever, but the underlying tension was gone. She felt a bit sad and upset with herself for taking so long to realize Dr. Carlos was the cause of it all.

By the look of things, two other doctors were stepping up to the plate in order to keep the ward running smoothly. This area of the hospital definitely seemed to not have a problem any longer. The Board would look over the candidates for Mario's job sometime next week. Based on her recommendations, she hoped they would make the leadership roles fall on a doctor and an RN. Balance would be better than chaos any day.

Now she fought the urge to run to her car. Julia waited for her, in need of quality play time. But first, there was her punishment to consider. It must be enough, so she learned from her mistakes, but also enough to bring her great pleasure in the end. Carmen's mind raced as her black Mercedes sped along the freeway. What should they start off with tonight? A smile slowly formed over her pink rose colored lips. The paddles and riding crop would prime Julia for an evening she wouldn't soon forget, but the thought of being able to play with her sub for an entire week, made Carmen's body shudder with desire. Finally, her own wish to have Julia in her arms again was about to become a reality.

* * * *

Julia's phone chirped with another text message. Her stomach fluttered to see the text from Mistress.

"Bath, black robe and box #4."

Julia's thighs immediately became slick with her juices. "Mistress wishes to use the paddles!" She scurried back to the bathroom to prepare the tub with Carmen's favorite rosemary and lavender bath salts. She adjusted the temperature to near scalding. She knew her Mistress loved the water hot and by the time she arrived, Julia hoped it would be the appropriate temperature.

Well, maybe not. If she got it wrong, she would receive more work with the paddles. If she guessed incorrectly, Mistress could withhold that and just let her suffer without release. No, it'd be better to follow the instructions to the letter and take the punishment and correction already in store for her.

She laid two more fluffy towels and a large black robe near the tub then zipped around as fast as the boots would allow, the bells jingling with every step and sway of her body. The clamps tugged at her tender flesh, sending more hot sensations racing through the rest of her body. She knew by the time Mistress arrived, she would be near exploding. The very thing expected of her, along with presenting herself with her hands clasped behind her back, breasts out, head up and eyes cast down. For the initial 'inspection', she could be standing but after that she may be required to crawl on her hands and knees. Once again her body shuddered. "Why the hell did I stay away so long? I need this. I need Carmen's firm hand and soft lips. I need to give myself over completely to her and never leave again."

The front door opened and closed with a soft thud. "Kitten? Are you ready for me?"

Julia cleared her now dry throat. "Yes, Mistress." *I'm ready to finally give you my heart!*

* * * *

Carmen entered the master bedroom, struck by the beauty of her sub. Stripped of all the trappings of her busy celebrity life, she appeared vulnerable and never more beautiful. She longed for this day for ages and her heart raced wildly. As Carmen approached, a soft jingling of the bells began. *Was she trembling?* "Kitten? Did you find everything I requested?" She put her fingertips under Julia's chin and lifted it—their signal, giving her permission to look into Carmen's eyes when she answered.

Julia's long lashes fluttered a bit before she complied.

Carmen felt very pleased to see Julia hadn't put in those damn colored contacts tonight. She preferred her kitten's steely gray eyes with flecks of amber which seemed to dazzle and dance when she became highly aroused, like now. "Yes, Ma'am. I placed the paddles on the dressing table along with your collection of chains and whips. The bath is ready with your favorite salts."

The bells sounded again, causing a rush of warmth between Carmen's legs. Normally, she stood taller than Julia, but with the five inch heels, they were nearly the same height now. Desire flooded through her as well as pride in her sub. She reached up and pulled the banana clip from her hair, allowing her mane to cascade down her back. Her lips touched Julia's slightly, eliciting a soft whimper from her and more jingling. Carmen's tongue plunged past her lips, slipping, sliding and possessing her sub with one deep kiss. "Beautiful."

Julia swooned slightly, giving in to the kiss completely.

Carmen trembled a bit herself, trembling with need to take Julia into her arms and never let go. "Do you have any idea how often I've fantasized you'd return here to me this way, kitten?"

Julia's eyes never wavered as they filled with tears. "Yes, Mistress. I've stayed away too long. I've come to beg for your forgiveness."

"Forgive you for what my darling pet?"

"Please forgive your kitten, Mistress for denying what her heart and body desired the most in the world."

Carmen's breath caught in her throat. *Could she really be admitting her true feelings tonight?* "Go on. What have you denied yourself?"

Julia trembled in her arms and more tears flowed down her cheeks. "I've denied my place with you. I've allowed others into my heart and bed when all along it's been you, Carmen—Mistress. If you'll still have me and find me worthy, I wish to stay here with you."

Carmen smiled and kissed Julia again, softly before pulling back, gazing deep into her eyes. "Nothing would please me more. Are you sure, Julia? I won't force you or beg you to stay with me. If you choose us now, it's forever."

Julia swallowed and managed to nod.

"Use your words, kitten."

"I love you. I can really be myself with you and in your care. You're the only one besides Jake who has ever loved me, and the only one who's never judged me. Punished me yes, but never judged."

* * * *

Chapter 26

Carmen held her breath as Julia slowly unbuttoned her dark green tailored dress shirt and slipped it from her shoulders. The bells jingled with each movement of her body, exciting and distracting Carmen. "Kneel, kitten. Put your hands behind your back."

"Yes, Mistress." Julia knelt before her, her tits pushed forward.

Carmen watched the blush slowly rise from those mounds and up toward her sub's cheeks. "You're right. I'll never judge you, but it is time for a bit of punishment. You've been quite generous with your sexual gifts over the years. Tell me, have you learned anything about yourself by doing that?" Carmen picked up the riding crop from the bedside table. "Look at me when you answer."

Julia did as instructed, slowly lifting her lids as tears trailed down her now rosy cheeks. "I've used my body to get what I wanted out of life. I didn't care who I hurt along the way."

"Why not?" Carmen tapped the bells hanging from Julia's nipples with the crop, eliciting a moan from her. "Not one of your lovers made you feel secure enough to drop your guard?"

"No, Mistress. I didn't allow myself to feel anything for anyone else until Jake."

Carmen's heart clenched. Guessing the truth was hard enough, but hearing it from her lover's lips was a bitter pill to swallow. "Why did you turn him away?"

"He wasn't you, Mistress. As much as he loved me, I couldn't give my heart to him. I do care for him deeply, but I tried to turn him into you." Julia hung her head and sobbed. "I didn't realize what I was doing until it went too far."

She tried to turn him into me? Carmen used the crop to tilt Julia's chin back up. "It's my fault as much as it's yours, kitten. You've been away for too long and I've neglected my duties as your Mistress." She gently wiped the tears from Julia's face and brushed her hair away from her face. "Bring me the paddle."

Julia bit her lower lip. "As you wish, Mistress." She slowly lowered herself to the floor and crawled to the bedside table. Using only her mouth, she took the paddle from the table and back toward Carmen. By the time she knelt and offered the paddle, Carmen already stripped off the remainder of her own clothing, except for her black lace bra and boy shorts.

Carmen took the paddle from Julia, before kissing her deeply. Teasing her tongue through her slightly parted lips sent a thrill through her body that Carmen didn't realize she'd missed. "Crawl to the ottoman and drape yourself over it, kitten."

Julia immediately dropped to the floor again, keeping her ass high in the air.

The paddle hit her right cheek with a loud crack. "A little higher, kitten." She struck Julia's round ass, making the left side as pink as the right. She hit her every step of the way, guiding her toward the leather ottoman in the opposite corner of the bedroom. With each contact, the bells attached to Julia's nipples and pussy answered with frantic jingles. The sound no longer distracted Carmen from her purpose, but encouraged her to keep going. Of course the moans coming from her beautiful sub added to her own mounting excitement. Her nipples tightened and her clit throbbed, but she put her needs to the back of her mind. "Spread your legs wider and lean all the way over so your hands are on the floor."

* * * *

Julia's ass burned from the paddle and yet she craved more. She knew her Mistress would deliver the appropriate punishment. She always knew what to do for her to give them both the greatest amount of pleasure. "Yes, Mistress." Julia placed her palms flat on the carpet, curled her fingers inward, and gripped the plush fibers as Carmen worked her with the paddle. A few times the edges of the paddle connected with her cunt sending jolts of pleasure and pain through her body, igniting the passion she hadn't felt in a long time. This was definitely where she belonged, with her Mistress, her true soul mate.

"You're going to get to know this paddle well, my sweet, but not all tonight. We've plenty of time together and I've a lot of instruction planned for you." Carmen slipped her fingers between Julia's pussy lips. "So wet for me already, kitten. Do you know how much that pleases me?"

"I'll do anything to please you." Julia thrust back toward Carmen as her fingers slid over her clit and then quickly withdrew. "Please don't stop, Mistress."

Carmen laughed softly as she rubbed soothing cream with her soft hands over Julia's thighs and bottom. "Don't you worry, there's going to be plenty of time for you to come for me, my love. Since it's been such a long time, your skin isn't used to being worked, but it will be."

Shivers flew up and down Julia's spine. The combination of the heat from the paddle, the coolness of the cream, and the touch of Carmen's hands became almost too much to take, and yet it was exactly what she needed and longed for from the very start. She felt a tug on her outer lips as the bell clamps were removed and cream worked into the skin where they'd been for the last few hours. Julia moaned again as Carmen spread her ass cheeks and slipped two fingers into her tight opening, coating her with the cream and stretching her with each feathering stroke.

Carmen picked up the crop with the special latex covered handle and bulb at the tip. It resembled a long, thick cock and was in fact, one of Julia's favorite toys.

Tonight she would be reacquainted with it. Just the sight of it made her body ache with need. The feel of the dildo sliding between her cheeks, sent a flood of her juices down her inner thighs with nothing she could do about it. She couldn't hold it back any longer and hoped it wouldn't displease her Mistress too much. A smile slowly formed on her lips thinking about what would happen next if Carmen followed her usual routine.

The bulb of the handle slowly slid passed the initial resistance to embed deep within her. Julia's clit throbbed in response to the fullness of the crop buried in her ass, and her hips rocked. She ground her pussy into the ottoman, attempting to give her clit some relief.

Carmen wasn't going to allow it however. "Kneel up, hands behind your back, kitten." She helped Julia get up and into position before shoving the crop a little deeper into her. "Now, I'm going to enjoy that hot bath you prepared for me. Keep your hands behind your back, legs apart, and that fake cock right where it is until I tell you otherwise. Are you okay with that or do you need a break, my pet?"

Julia swallowed hard and licked her lips. "I could use a drink of water, Mistress."

Carmen held a bottle of water with a straw while Julia drained nearly half of it in three gulps.

"Thank you."

Carmen kissed her forehead and then her lips softly. "I won't be long and then we'll start again. I was thinking of our last session after you visited me today. We had such a short time together then, not enough to really see what both of us were made of. But this time, oh honey, this time we are going to be able to let everything and everyone else go."

* * * *

Chapter 27

The bath eased away the remaining tension from Carmen's body. Julia timed it just right. It still remained steaming hot when she left her kitten alone in the bedroom. By the time she finished her flesh looked rosy pink, just like Julia's ass after their paddle work. Carmen felt happy with her sub's progress and even happier she'd finally found her true self after all these years.

On one of their first trips to Hawaii, Julia confided in her about the abuse she suffered at the hands of both of her parents. Julia's step-father felt it was his *right* to fuck his preteen daughter whenever his common law wife was 'indisposed'. Julia's mother made sure she remained in an indisposed condition on a regular basis, once her daughter reached puberty. Hell, the skank even participated in the sessions as Julia called them. Carmen asked her why she never called it for what it's been—sexual abuse. She would just shrug her shoulders and say it'd been what she thought life was supposed to be like back then.

When Julia finally realized it wasn't normal to have her father fuck her up the ass and her mother give her pointers on how to perform blow jobs, she was out of there and on the first bus traveling to California. Ever since then, Julia never enjoyed oral sex with a man unless she was on the receiving end. Each time she tried, she would hear her mother's voice in her head telling her what she was doing wrong. It just seemed to be easier to never do the oral sexual act again. So far, the only one who's ever complained about seemed to be Mario. No matter now. He was no longer in the picture and for that, Carmen felt extremely grateful.

She never asked Julia about her past again. She didn't want to bring up anymore horrible memories for her, and she became determined to protect her from any of it coming back to haunt her. Julia changed her entire identity on the long bus ride from Missouri to California. As far as anyone else was concerned, little Julianna Marshall no longer existed. She became Julia Santos, artist, and the best damn sub Carmen ever dominated. In fact, she ended up being the best thing to ever come into her life and the only person who possessed her heart.

Watching Julia kneel silently next to the ottoman, the crop still buried deep in her ass, Carmen knew she'd found her perfect companion, the ying to her yang. She wanted nothing more than to shout it to the world, but there would be plenty of time for that later. First, she needed to tend to her sub. She crossed the room in just four strides, dropped her black robe to the floor, and stood naked before her lover. "You've been a very obedient slave, my darling."

With gentle tugs, Carmen removed the bell clamps from Julia's nipples, rubbing more cream into the pinched, tender skin.

Julia sighed and shivered slightly, but overall kept still.

"Come over to the bed and lie on your stomach for me." Without any further instructions, Julia crawled across the floor to the king sized bed and draped herself over the end, ass in the air. The crop phallus, still firmly implanted in her, swayed as she adjusted herself, keeping her legs spread apart. Carmen stood behind her and caressed Julia's thighs. "Relax, kitten. I'm going to remove your adornment and then your boots."

"Yes, Mistress." She braced herself and gripped the bedspread tightly. Carmen eased the crop out in one fluid motion, planting kisses on Julia's lower back and both of her ass cheeks. Julia pushed back against her, lifting her hips higher to expose her glistening pussy lips.

Carmen's mouth watered as Julia's scent filled her nose, making her light headed with desire. She quickly unzipped and removed both boots from Julia's shapely legs, resisting the urge to slip between those thighs to suck on her clit. "Roll over and lay back on the pillows, love."

Julia hesitated and didn't move immediately.

That earned her one, two and three swift slaps of Carmen's bare hands on her bottom. "Now!"

* * * *

Julia's face burned. She hated not knowing what was expected of her, and she'd been momentarily caught off guard. Normally, Carmen would've kept her leaning over the bed while she ravaged Julia's cunt with her mouth, fingers and a few toys. The change in their old routine made a bit of doubt creep into her mind.

What if I can't do what Carmen's asks of me this time? Will she toss me out and never want to see me again? Fear of failure caused her to hesitate and incur the spanking. Julia needed to stay focused on Carmen's voice. Finally, she did what she was told and settled back at the top of the bed on the pillows.

Before she could apologize for not moving sooner, Carmen's lips were on hers, nearly taking her breath away with the intensity of her kiss. Her hands pinned Julia's high above her head, preventing her from doing anything but give in completely to her Mistress. Carmen's tongue slid passed Julia's lips with ease, possessing hers completely before tearing away to zero in on her neck just below her ear.

Julia moaned and wrapped her legs around Carmen's ample hips. She kissed her back hard, not caring if she was overstepping her role as sub or if it earned her another punishment. She wanted Carmen and she wanted her now.

Her lover seemed to sense the change in her and chuckled softly before freeing Julia's hands. Carmen slid down her body, licking and sucking everything in her path.

The licking set Julia's skin ablaze with each contact. "Please, Mistress. I want to taste you too." Her voice sounded foreign to her, soft and a little hoarse with need. Never before did she beg anyone and actually mean it.

Carmen unhooked Julia's legs from around her hips and pulled her down along the bed.

Now she lay flat against the mattress, no pillows under her.

Carmen slid back up toward the top of the bed and straddled Julia's body, her pussy hovering just inches above her mouth. "Is *this* what you want, kitten? You want to bury your face in my cunt?"

Julia's body shivered. "Oh god, yes Mistress. Please let me bury my tongue inside your hot pussy."

Carmen slowly lowered herself the last bit.

Julia couldn't hold back any longer. Her tongue darted in and out of Carmen's slit, lapping up some of her sweet juices before honing in on her target. Carmen gasped and jumped slightly when her lips found her clit, but Julia held her firmly in place, nails digging slightly into her ass while she fucked her with her tongue. With each thrust, more juices gushed out of Carmen and coated Julia's lips and chin. The mix of the jasmine and rosemary bath salts and the natural musky odor of high arousal, made Carmen smell and taste irresistible to Julia. The more that flowed from her, the more she wanted to take.

"Oh my god, baby! Don't stop!" Carmen ground her pussy against Julia's mouth and hands as she fucked her with two then three fingers, feathering her hot walls until she screamed out Julia's name. She fell forward to rest on top of her lover's body, appearing as if she were completely drained.

Julia knew better.

Immediately, Carmen latched onto Julia's clit, sucked hard and flicked it repeatedly with her tongue.

"Yes, Mistress. Make your kitten come again for you." Julia moaned against Carmen's pussy as the other lapped up all of her cream and worked to bring out more, darting her tongue in and out of her folds while her thumb continued to rub Julia's clit.

Each worked the other until they reached the peak together, clinging to each other as their bodies shuddered through their release.

Carmen rolled off Julia and turned to lie at the top of the bed. Settling on the pillows, she held her arms open, beckoning to Julia to come join her.

Julia crawled up next to her and laid her head on Carmen's shoulder. She closed her eyes, allowing her breathing to slow and normalize.

Carmen wrapped her arms around her and kissed her forehead before tilting her chin up to make it easier to kiss her softly on her swollen lips. "I've waited so long for this day to happen. I still can't believe you're here with me again."

Julia hugged Carmen tighter. "I *am* here with you now and forever if you'll have me, Carmen. I know I've got a long way to prove it to you, but I love you and I want to spend the rest of my life with you."

Carmen fell quiet, almost too quiet for Julia's taste and it scared her more than a little. She sat up and searched the face of the woman she loved for any clues as to what she might be thinking or feeling. Julia's heart nearly stopped until she saw that beautiful smile she adored so much forming on Carmen's lips.

"I love you too, Julia. You don't have anything to prove to me. The fact that you're here now means the world to me. Nothing and no one else matters but that."

"Do you mean it? You forgive me for wasting so much time with other lovers when we could have had this from day one?"

"There's nothing to forgive. You had to fly on your own before you could be able to know for sure this is what you wanted. You had to be the one to choose. I would never force you to be someone you can't be. When we first met, there was no way you were ready for this. You still needed to figure out who you are. I think you've done that, thanks to Jake. He helped you see that there are people who can love you for you and not as a possession."

Julia hung her head. "I never wanted to hurt him and if I could go back and change things, I don't think I would've chased after him two years ago. I was just as bad to him as others have been to me in my life. I treated him like a pet. Yes I loved him and really got off on his unconditional love for me, but in the end, I knew I could never be what he wanted me to be and he couldn't be you."

"One day I'll have to thank Mr. Hartley."

"For what?"

"For helping you find your way back to yourself and to me." She pulled Julia back down on the pillows and kissed her again.

Julia touched Carmen's flushed cheek with her fingertips. "I have a long way to go to find *me* again. I'm going to need your help to find a therapist I can trust. I can't keep running from my past."

Carmen smiled. "I've already lined up a few for you to interview. It's important you feel comfortable with them so you can confront your demons. I'll be with you every step of the way."

Julia clung to her, so happy to be in the arms of the only person she's ever given her heart to for safe keeping. "No matter what comes out?"

"No matter what. I didn't answer your question before." Carmen rested her forehead against the top of Julia's head and her smile widened.

Julia shook her head. She reached up and brushed a few stray blonde curls behind Carmen's ear. "No, I don't think you did."

"The answer is yes. I will have you now and forever."

* * * *

Lady Fate stood with Daniel watching over the two women. "What has you so troubled, Daniel?"

"I'm not troubled, but more like flabbergasted. At first I wasn't too keen on the idea you wanted me to watch over this one. She seemed to be too far gone down the chaotic path to turn back."

"And now?" Fate tilted her head and smiled. "Has she passed your tests?"

Daniel blushed. "Well, I've learned to never judge a book by its cover when it comes to what Destiny has in store for anyone. Julia went through hell as a child. It's a wonder she didn't turn out just as sadistic as her parents."

"A wonder indeed. Lucius threw a lot of trials and tribulations her way and she got through them all the best she could. She's earned her right to a happily ever after too."

"She has really turned a corner and with Carmen by her side, I think Julia will start to accept she deserves to be happy. I don't know if the Hartley family would see it that way though." Daniel shook his head slowly. "It looks to them and many other people as if she was the cause for Jake's accident."

Fate nodded. "She played a major roll, yes. But you have to remember it was all at Lucius's hand. He uses whatever and whoever He feels necessary to test Our creations. Whether they pass or fail these trials will determine which paths they end up on and which destiny they will get this lifetime."

Daniel smiled and projected his angelic light toward Carmen and Julia.

Fate raised her eyebrow. "Who needed the healing this time?"

"It's for both of them. In order for Julia to completely give her heart to Carmen, she's going to have to relive some of the horrors from her past and let them go completely. Hearing Julia's life story, all of it, is going to shake Carmen to her core. She'll even have to come to grips with the reality that there are truly evil people in the world and make her question her own choices in life and her career. They'll need each other more than ever then. I just wanted to give them a little nudge to let them know they'll get through it all together."

The Goddess laughed. "A little nudge can go a long way. We definitely chose the right Guardian this time. Julia and Carmen are now moving in the right direction and with you to watch over them, I'm sure their happiness will know no bounds."

Daniel smiled and lowered his head while bowing slightly.

"Come now, Daniel. I would like to check in on a few more of our couples before you head back to the Island."

"Where to next?"

"Your cousin, Samantha's broken heart has called out to me. She's been in love with her Michael since they were in high school, no?"

Daniel nodded. "Unfortunately, he seems to break her heart over and over again. Each time she forgives him and lets him back in her life. I wish she would find someone else to give her love to, someone who would cherish it more."

"I have just the person. Your partner is with him now. He's had to deal with more than his fair share of Lucius's tests lately, but he's pulled himself through nicely."

"Do you mean Nathan? Mike's Marine Corps buddy?" Daniel knit his eyebrows together. "I'll trust your judgment here, since I don't know much about him. When do you want to visit Sammi?"

Fate laughed. "Well, no time like the present!"

Chapter 28

February 13th, Present Day, Las Vegas

"Dr. Hall's flight landed only moments ago. It's going to take her a few minutes to make it through the terminal down here to baggage claim. If you keep pacing like that, you're gonna wear down those fancy heels of yours before you get to see her." Darryl smiled

Julia immediately felt the tension leave her body.

"Now that's better."

Julia laughed and slid her hand around the driver's arm and held on tight. "I'm just so excited that she was able to get away much sooner than expected. This means we can do a bit of exploring together before we go to the House of Blues tonight."

"Quarter to Three puts on a mighty fine show. My daughter's dating the drummer, you know." Darryl winked and patted her hand. "Rumor has it Derek can't wait to meet you in person. He's asked me to give you a few subtle hints about stopping in to see him this afternoon concerning a tattoo for each of you."

"Did he now? I've only talked to him on the phone to inquire about designing matching tats. I hadn't set up any specific appointment yet because I wasn't sure when Carmen could join me here. It just so happens, I told Jake and Quinn this morning we would meet them there after I get Carmen settled in at the hotel. I want to surprise her with matching tattoos to celebrate my new venture with Mr. Eischer." She scanned the crowd looking for her lover and frowned when she didn't see her curly blond hair anywhere in the throng of travelers.

"Well, Derek's creations are beautiful. You can't ask for anyone better. All of the guys at his shop are extremely talented artists and I have a few from each of them myself. I think part of the excitement of having one of them work on you is sitting in the chair while all those folks outside the shop look on through the glass walls." He patted her hand and then pointed toward the group just coming down the escalator. "I do believe that's Dr. Hall, making her way down now."

Julia looked in the direction he pointed and started waving and bouncing on her toes. "That's her! Carmen!" Julia didn't care what anyone else thought of a forty-something year old woman squealing with delight in the middle of baggage claim. She bolted through the group of people separating them and threw herself into her lover's open arms.

Carmen spun her around a few times before letting her go. She smiled at Darryl before turning her attention back to Julia. "I'm happy to see you too, kitten but how about you introduce me to your hunky companion."

Julia blushed. "I'm sorry. Carm, this is my good luck charm, Darryl. He's here to make sure we get you to MGM in one piece."

"Hello, Darryl. I've heard quite a bit about you already. Anyone who can calm Julia's nerves about coming out here is definitely a friend of mine."

He took her small hand into both of his large ones and shook it warmly. "Welcome to Las Vegas, Dr. Hall. It's a pleasure to help Ms. Santos start a new adventure here. I look forward to seeing you both a lot now that she's agreed to be part of the MGM team."

Carmen raised her eyebrows and smiled. "Did she have any other choice, Darryl?"

A deep rumbling laugh filled Julia's ears. He tipped his hat at both women as he collected Carmen's luggage from the conveyor belt. "No, I guess not. When Mr. Eischer makes up his mind about something, it's pretty much a done deal. It's best to just go with it and let the chips fall where they may. It *is* Vegas after all."

Julia held Carmen's hand tightly as they walked toward the limo behind Darryl. "As soon as we get you all settled into the suite, I was hoping you'd come with me to meet Derek Quartermarsh at The Tattoo Parlor. Quinn and Jake will be there too."

"He's in town? Of course I'd love to meet him. Do you think he'd create a couple tats for us?" Carmen's eyes twinkled with her smile.

Julia's stomach fluttered. She loved being able to bring that smile to her Mistress's face. It's what she lived for and would give anything to see every single day. Carmen stuck by her through so many dark days over the years and could have left her on several occasions, but she never did. She'd said forever and she meant it.

"That was supposed to be one of the surprises I have in store for you over the next couple days, and Derek has agreed to design something that matches our personalities. I'm excited to see what he comes up with." The women followed Darryl out of the sliding doors and made their way to the limo parked at the curb.

"You said the tattoos were just one of the surprises for me. Just what have you been up to since you got into town?"

Julia smiled before settling back into the seat with her head on Carmen's shoulder. "My lips are sealed. You'll just have to wait to see what happens. Trust me. I think you'll like every single minute of it." She'd been determined to surprise her as much as possible during their stay. Carmen always took care of her every wish and whim, spoiling her absolutely rotten at times. Now it was her turn to do the spoiling and Julia really looked forward to it all.

Thanks to Carmen she found herself at a point in her life where she could talk about her past—all of it, and not just the select bits and pieces she chose to let people know about. It'd been bad enough, telling her about the sexual abuse by her parents, but when she finally told her the rest of it, Julia felt sure Carmen would call it quits. Not only did her parents use her as their own toy, they sold her every week to their lowlife friends. Nothing seemed off the table if they had enough money to pay. One agreed to pay her parents three hundred dollars to be able the fuck her wherever he wanted and however he wanted for a full twenty-four hours. Never mind she'd only been fourteen years old at the time, because she looked like she was at least eighteen. At the end of her time with him, he handed her an additional two hundred bucks. He winked at her and told her there'd be more where that came from as long as she would be his whenever he came to town.

Any normal girl would have refused his indecent, immoral and *oh so illegal* proposal, but not Julia. She'd learned to turn inside herself when she needed to perform for her parents and their friends. The little girl longing to have parents who loved her and protected her from all the monsters became too broken to stay in control any longer. It'd been the first time Julia Santos took over completely. With the money clutched tightly in her fist, it set her free and buried the other weaker Julia, so nothing could ever harm her again.

Afterward, she met that man nearly every week, giving her parents the money they demanded as payment for her services, and pocketing the rest for herself. This went on for several months, keeping both of her parents happy for a change. In young Julia's mind, her life was going pretty good if her step-father left her alone and the extra money kept coming in.

Unfortunately, her mother found her stash of money a few months later and blew it all on booze for herself and her lowlife husband. Well, not all of it. Some of it went to pay for Julia's medical bills. Instead of taking her to get proper medical care when she inevitably did get pregnant, Julia's mother took her to a friend of a friend's doctor who performed the abortion for just a few hundred bucks. Because of that quack, Julia was scarred so badly she'd been told later by her doctors in California, she would never be able to conceive a child of her own, let alone carry one to term.

Just one more thing the people who called themselves her parents stole from her.

Her grandmother did the best she could by her, God rest her sweet soul. While in the old woman's presence Julia would allow the innocent one to come back out. It became the only safe place for her to do so. The night before her sixteenth birthday was one of those times. The innocent Julianna got on that bus to California after a tearful goodbye to the only family she ever loved. It'd been the tough as nails Julia Santos who got off the bus when it finally arrived in Los Angeles.

It took a lot of therapy for Julia to even acknowledge that part of her past ever happened let alone share it with Carmen. How do you tell the woman you love that your parents sold you to their friends every week and you made side deals with these men for extra money? How do you tell the one you love about how you needed to create an entirely different personality in order to cope with all of it and survive? How could you tell anyone the reason you shied away from being around children wasn't because you didn't like them, but because it hurt too much to know you'd never be able to have one of your own?

Julia learned at a young age she loved sex and the power she could hold over the people who wanted it from her. It wasn't until Jacob's accident when Julia saw how that behavior almost destroyed her and the sweet child she'd kept hidden, deep inside her soul. She couldn't blame it all on her dirt bag parents. She needed to take control of her life. She chose to be a manipulative bitch as an adult and use sex in order to control everyone around her.

No one forced her to do anything anymore. She chose to give up the hedonistic lifestyle she once thought fulfilled all her needs, wants and desires. Daniel and the Goddess Fate showed her it wasn't too late to turn her life around. Her time on the Island gave her the courage to face her demons and finally escape them once and for all.

Now that she'd made amends to Jacob, she could concentrate on her relationship with Carmen and to giving her all the happiness she deserved and then some.

"Honey, where did you go just now? I've been chattering nonstop about my flight and you've not uttered a peep." Carmen kissed her forehead and hugged her tight against her.

"Just thinking about everything you've put up with from me over the years. I want this trip to be the start of our future together, guilt free. Jake said he forgave me a long time ago and thanks to Steve Eischer, I'm entering a new phase in my career. For the first time in a hell of a lot of years, I can finally see our happily ever after. Will you go on this journey with me?"

Carmen put her fingertips under Julia's chin and gently tilted her face upward. "I wouldn't want to be anywhere else. Have you any idea how happy you've made me today?"

"Well, I hope to make you even happier before this week is over." The limo pulled up to the MGM private parking area reserved for the staff and Steve's special guests. "Come on. Let's get your things upstairs and freshen up a bit before I show you around. This place is fascinating and I have so many ideas for the club."

"Lead the way, kitten. Lead the way."

* * * *

Carmen sat in Derek's chair first, while Julia chatted with Jacob and Quinn's cousin Brigid. Watching the love of her life laughing and bouncing a baby on her knee, nearly brought tears to her eyes. She couldn't hear all of their conversation, but she felt the positive energy throughout the shop and it absolutely thrilled her to no end. Just last year, Julia felt terrified to see Jacob again. Now she planned for them to go out with him and his wife to a concert tonight. The biggest surprise to Carmen was how comfortable Julia appeared around the twins. All the years she's known her, this would be the very first time Carmen ever saw her partner smiling and actually enjoying herself around kids.

"It's amazing to watch people come full circle isn't it?" Derek finished setting up his inks and moved his chair closer to hers. "Two years ago, I didn't think we'd ever see Quinn or Jake smile again, let alone be celebrating their anniversary."

She smiled and turned to look into his eyes, lowering her voice so the others wouldn't overhear. "Yes it is. I've prayed for this to happen for Julia for so long, but honestly I was beginning to wonder if we would ever get to this point."

Derek nodded. "You and me both, Doc. This is the perfect time for the two of you to be here in Vegas, you know. It's not always easy to get the entire Hartley clan together in one place. This way Julia can make amends with Katrina and Maredyth now too." He continued to work the outline of the phoenix on her upper back.

The design would be exactly what Julia described to him over the phone. Besides the bright purples, greens and blues of the creature itself, Derek added a few extra bits to the design to symbolize both women. In one claw it clutched a black flogger, and the other a set of handcuffs. When he showed them the design, he chuckled at their shocked expressions before showing his own dominatrix tattoo on his right hip. He then explained his fiancé wore a matching one on her left hip, both courtesy of one of the other guys in the shop.

Carmen was tickled to learn the rock star she'd been all fan girl over shared the same lifestyle as she did. The trip just kept getting better and better.

"Besides Jake, Mrs. Hartley is the one she'd been most afraid to meet. I mean, how to you tell someone you're sorry for nearly killing their son?"

"He didn't die, now did he? He got to be on the Island with Quinn all those years ago. It set the stage for them to find each other again now. And by the looks of things, I'd say she's finally accepting that fact, wouldn't you?" Derek stopped for a few moments to change to another color before continuing to fill in the body of the mythical creature representing so much to both Carmen and Julia.

"I've never seen her so happy. She's positively glowing and has been since she picked me up at the airport. You're right. This was the best time for her to be here. I'm just happy I could fly in a few days earlier than I originally planned. I get to witness her enter a new phase of her life and I get to see you and Quarter to Three perform again. I couldn't ask for anything more."

Julia glanced up and smiled broadly. "You wait. I've got a few more things planned for us tonight yet, and then there's Jake and Quinn's anniversary party tomorrow."

Quinn stepped out of the back room carrying her daughter in one arm and a diaper bag slung over the other. "And we won't take no for an answer either, Carmen."

Derek laughed. "Don't fight it. My sister will hound you until you say yes. She learned the technique from Steve Eischer."

Carmen shook her head and smiled. "Well, if it means so much to all of you, how can I possibly say no? I can't very well come to the biggest adult playground in the world and be the one and only party-pooper, can I?"

Julia got up from the waiting area and took the seat next to Carmen, reaching for her hand before kissing her softly on the lips. "No you can't. It's my turn to show you just how much you mean to me, and this place, this fabulous city is the perfect setting. It is Vegas after all."

* * * *

Chapter 29

"Wow, will you look at this crowd! I knew Quarter to Three had a following, but I thought Steve said tonight's show was more for friends and family." Carmen's grip on Julia's fingers tightened ever so slightly as they made their way through the crowd toward the tables in front of the stage.

Julia smiled. "Well, one thing I've learned over the last few days is Steve's idea of just family and friends means practically the entire state of Nevada. Most of the folks here tonight are either friends or relatives of Jake, Quinn, or the guys in Derek's band."

Eric helped both of them with their seats and sat next to Carmen. "Derek and the guys have been playing together for over ten years now. They've quite a following here and every once in a while they like to perform for those who've been with them from the beginning. We're in for an extra special treat. Brigid's going to join the band onstage tonight. Derek said her voice is a cross between Adele and Melissa Etheridge."

"Now I'm really glad I was able to get out here so soon. Carmen's face positively glowed with excitement as she looked around the room.

Julia loved to see her so relaxed and happy. Their life together had been filled with many ups and downs up until this point, many of them because of her therapy. Having Carmen here in Las Vegas now seemed like perfect timing. Julia wanted to kick off the rest of their future together with a bang and the concert at the House of Blues would be just the beginning.

Julia smiled at Katrina Hartley as Steve helped her with her seat. They officially met only a few hours before and she still felt surprised by all of it. For years, she'd been terrified of coming face to face with Jacob's mother but when the time came, the woman made her feel like one of her long lost children.

She immediately pulled her into a bear hug as soon as they were introduced by Eric. Before she could get in a word edgewise, Katrina told her she'd forgiven her long ago because her husband told her the entire story. Julia felt stunned to learn about Michael Hartley continuing to watch over his family and the fact that Katrina could see him. Until she met with Jacob and Quinn, she'd actually started to believe her therapist's idea about the visits to the Island, Danny, Michael and Lady Fate were all part of her own mind.

Now she knew for a fact all of it really happened and it just made her more determined to make this night extra special for her Mistress. She's seen her through so much and never left her side. Now it was Julia's turn to make a few more of her fantasies come true. She worked out a few requests with Derek and Brigid in order to keep the surprises coming. Only one other person knew of the extra special gift she'd procured for Carmen.

Everyone else thought they were there to celebrate the success of the band's last tour, but it'd been Quinn who suggested they turn it into something more. Julia felt reluctant at first, but after talking to Quinn and

Katrina, she agreed to do it. Now she needed to wait for the perfect time in the evening to move forward with her plans.

Speaking of other plans, it became apparent to Julia her new employer might just be a bit smitten with one of the women who traveled with Quinn's family to Vegas.

Katie seemed to be another one of those classic beauties to catch Julia's artistic eye. With her curly brown hair piled up on top of her head, leaving soft tendrils framing her face and tickling her neck. Her green eyes seemed to be her best trait and they made Julia's creative brain go into overdrive. The same eyes she'd wanted to make the centerpiece of one of the portraits she'd do for Saints and Sinners, and she didn't think she'd have trouble convincing Steve to let her do it either.

Even deep in conversation with the others at their table, his eyes were continually drawn to the Irish beauty seated across from him at the neighboring table. By the blush coloring her fair cheeks, it became evident Katie was taken with Steve as well. *Vegas is definitely a place where sparks fly. No wonder Jake and Quinn wanted to move back here. This town is simply magical!"*

* * * *

At the table just to the right of the stage, Daniel Quartermarsh looked on, as his cousin Brigid took command of the crowd. It'd been a few years since she'd performed with any band, instead concentrating full time on her catering business with Katie and his sister Miranda.

The roar of the crowd sent chills up and down his spine. Before his death, he loved every single moment of performing onstage with his own band. Music and family were his life then, but now there were other responsibilities he wouldn't trade for anything. He could enjoy watching his cousin and Derek in the spotlight now. Every beat of the drum and every chord from the guitars hummed through him and warmed his soul.

Even though he'd become an angel, he still experienced all of it again as a spectator in his materialized form. His partner Michael Hartley joined him after grabbing a beer from the bar for both of them. Tonight would be a special night and they were allowed to celebrate with a bit of their former indulgences. To the rest of the club patrons, they looked like any other party there to enjoy the concert, but a few saw them for who they really were. Brigid, Katrina, and Steve were the only ones who caught on right away, but the angel felt sure they wouldn't say anything until the time seemed right.

Daniel watched Fate take a small sip of the strawberry daiquiri Lucius brought for her to try and then laughed as she then took a strong pull from the straw. "I take it you find your drink acceptable?"

"Oh yes. I should try these a bit more often. Now I know why Lucius loves to hang out in places like this. The excitement here tonight makes my heart very happy. To see nearly all of your charges here celebrating with each other is well worth the energy it takes to keep all of us in human form, and yes I do love these icy drinks."

The God of Trials and Tribulations chuckled. "Sister, if you drink that any faster you're not going to be able to hold your stunning human form much longer." He pushed the drink away from her toward the center of the table, eliciting a small pout from her. "You can have that back after we talk about a few things. It appears everything is going according to plan for Julia and Carmen and a new twist has developed with Katie's appearance sooner than expected."

Daniel squirmed slightly in his seat. "That would be our doing. Michael and I intervened a bit on behalf of my cousin Sammi and Steve's friend Nathan. We felt it was necessary for her to be here with him now to secure their relationship. They're going to need each other for some rough patches ahead."

"And Katie is here to encourage Samantha to explore her attraction to Nathan?" Lucius raised one eyebrow and smiled. "I see my sister's hand in this as well."

The Goddess blushed a bit. "You do know me very well, brother dear. Of course I encouraged the intervention. Her heart has been broken too many times by Katie's brother, Mike. Both women have suffered because of him and it's time each enjoyed themselves a bit. Is it so wrong to pair up the couples I know are meant to be?"

"It is if it's too soon to do it. But don't worry. I'm on your side in this case. There's still more for all of them to go through before they can completely give their hearts to each other like Quinn and Jacob, but it's a damn good start." Lucius couldn't keep his eyes off the stage as soon as Brigid started belting out her next tune. Daniel never heard her sound so soulful and yes, a bit raunchy with a song by one of Quinn's favorite artists. Maybe it wasn't such a good idea to sing lyrics which included the words *slut like you* in the chorus, but it made the crowd jump up on their feet, including his mother and Katrina. Her charms also affected the immortals, especially Lucius. She'd gotten his full attention now.

Fate giggled. "Our Brigid is a fiery creature and one of the few humans who could ever resist your charms. It's obvious from your reaction tonight, she's as the humans say, *under your skin."*

Lucius grinned. "She won't be resisting me for much longer. I think I'm finally starting to wear her down."

Daniel raised his eyebrows in surprise. "Can I ask what you mean by that?"

Lucius's laughter rung in his ears and immediately put him at ease. "I have nothing but good intentions toward your cousin. In fact, she just may be as you say, 'it'...for me."

Fate nearly choked on her drink then turned her brilliant emerald eyes on the younger god. "Are you sure? Once the choice is made, it cannot be undone." She bit her lip to hide the smile that threatened to come into view.

Lucius continued to watch Brigid on stage and kept silent, ignoring his sister's teasing.

"What does Yeshua say about this?"

"Haven't brought it up yet. We've all been a wee bit preoccupied with the rest of this bunch." Lucius signaled to the waitress to bring over another round of drinks to the table.

Michael nodded. "I agree. This group has been quite the challenge. I can also understand why you've taken a liking to Brigid. She's the perfect match for you and your brooding ways. From the way she talks about you stalking her, I would say she's a bit enamored of you as well. Keep it up. I don't think you'll have to wait much longer for her to fall head over heels for you...if she hasn't done so already." He winked at Daniel before excusing himself to get a little bit closer to his family. He dematerialized as he walked into the crowd and then settled in next to his wife and Jacob.

Fate turned to Daniel and waved him on. "Go ahead. Your family's waiting. Brigid has prepared Derek, so you can share the experience on stage with him tonight. It's his gift to your family. Only they'll be able to see you there. Everyone else will see Derek."

"One last song with Quinn and Brig?" He hadn't dared to hope he'd be allowed to do this. It was usually not allowed for the Guardians to interact with their charges this way.

The Goddess nodded. "You deserve it after all your hard work bringing these couples together."

Daniel didn't need to be told twice. In a flash he faded to his angelic form and appeared on stage next to Derek.

Brigid nodded when she spotted him... "Are you ready?" she whispered so only Derek could hear.

He smiled and nodded. "Come on up here and join us, Quinn. We've one more special request to do." Under his breath he continued, "Anytime you're ready, brotha."

Daniel stepped forward and merged with Derek as his back was turned to the crowd. When he turned around again, he caught his mother's eye and winked. The look on Helen Quartermarsh's face told him all he wanted to know. She could see him and so could his sister Miranda and her husband Robb. Quinn flashed him a smile and took her place at the drums while Brigid took over the keyboards, giving some of the band a break.

He cleared his throat tentatively, trying out the new body and vocal cords. *This should be interesting!* "This song is one of our favorites and has special meaning to many in the room tonight." Daniel gently strummed his guitar as the others settled into place. There they were again, on stage one last time, thanks to a gift from The Three. "When you're lost and don't know which way to turn, just listen to your heart. It will never steer you wrong."

Katrina reached for Jacob's hand and squeezed it tightly. Even on stage with the noise of the crowd surrounding him, Daniel could hear every single conversation. "Can you see? Both of our angels are here, Jacob."

"Yes, Ma. We can see. Pop and Danny are here." He leaned over and kissed her cheek then wrapped his arm around her, hugging her close.

Julia's eyes flew open in surprise. "Is that—?"

Steve reached for her free hand. "Danny? Yes it is. My guess his song tonight is especially for you and Carmen. If this isn't a sign that you're on the right track with your life now, I don't know what is."

Daniel didn't realize just how much he missed holding a guitar in his hands. He would forever be grateful to Derek for allowing him to do this. In his mind, he heard the musician's laughter. *Just relax. You know Brigid will lead you through all of this, but don't get too comfy in here. I'm gonna want my body back at some point tonight. I don't think my fiancé would take too kindly to sharing me with anyone else.*

As Brigid started the first chords of the song, everything melted away for Daniel except the music. Her soulful husky voice took command of the Roxette tune with ease. When they reached the first chorus, Daniel made sure to hold Julia's gaze with his own. "Listen to your heart. There's nothing else you can do."

The harmony between the three of them was spot on and nearly brought him to his knees. By the end of the song, there wasn't a dry eye in the house. Each and every person found their own message in the lyrics, but he knew it'd been Julia he needed to reach tonight to give her the encouragement she needed. He held her gaze a few moments longer then turned things back over to Derek. The last thing he saw while he left the stage was Julia mouthing the words...*"I will."*

* * * *

Fate stood next to her brother and slipped her arm through his. "I think it's our turn to leave. Daniel and Michael can handle things from here. I'm sure you'll be able to catch up with Brigid soon."

"You can be sure of that. She's one I can't stay away from even if I tried. Much like you with Julia and Carmen, I can't give up on her. Enough about me." He took a deep breath and exhaled slowly.

Fate knew he intended to make another confession to her and she wasn't sure if she felt ready to hear another shocking admittance by him, like perhaps thinking of giving up his immortality to be with a human.

"I just wanted to let you know I think you've made the right choice to intervene with Julia and Carmen at the same time you helped put Jacob and Quinn on the correct path. Those two needed more than a few nudges to get them together and they sure as hell didn't make it easy. You stuck to your guns and insisted that Yeshua agree with you, and I admire that. I don't know how you're able to see the good in so many. I wish I had even a fraction of that gift." He cleared his throat one more time before he said the words Fate thought she'd never hear from his lips. "As always, you've chosen the best Guardians for the job." He patted her hand as they slowly walked through the crowded music hall toward the exit.

The goddess stopped in her tracks and blushed once again. "Lucius, I don't think you've ever—"

He wrapped his arms around her and held her tight. "Shush. Keep your voice down. We can't let it get out that I'm passing out compliments. You'll ruin my street cred."

"Lucius! You're incorrigible." Fate's bawdy laughter faded as the Siblings left the casino and the Earth Realm. Leaving the destinies of their charges in their own hands wasn't easy for her to do, but she meant what she said.

The guardians could handle whatever this bunch tossed at them.

* * * *

Chapter 30

Julia turned to Carmen to see her wiping tears from her cheeks. She knew in her heart the moment she'd been waiting for had arrived. "I'm listening to my heart now, Carm." She reached inside her purse to pull out a red crushed velvet ring box and placed it on the table in front of them. "You've been by my side through some of the happiest times of my life and some of my darkest days. You never stopped believing I would find my way back to myself and to us."

Carmen opened the box to reveal the claddagh engagement rings Julia ordered months ago, hoping one day to be able to give them to her. The matching diamond and ruby rings glistened in the lighting from the stage, bringing fresh tears to her lover's eyes.

"My heart has always belonged to you and I'm finally in a place where I can give it to you freely, if you'll accept it and be my happily ever after." Julia got down on her knees before her Mistress one more time. "Will you marry me?"

The crowd in the concert hall went silent. No one even took a breath, least of all Julia, for fear of missing the answer to her question.

Carmen clutched Julia's hands so tightly, she thought she'd break a finger or two before she relaxed her grip. Slowly the megawatt smile that knocked her for a loop all those years ago emerged. "I've waited so long for you to see what I see in you and to finally believe you deserve to be loved. I only hoped one day you'd want me as much as I wanted you, and for you to see we belong to each other. You're as much a part of me as I am of you..."

Eric broke the silence. "Well? What do you say, Carm?"

Katrina slapped her youngest son on the arm. "Shush now. Let her speak."

Laughing through her tears, Carmen waited a few moments until it got quiet again. "Yes, of course I'll marry you, kitten. You're my heart, my soul, my everything." She stood up and pulled Julia from the floor, into her arms and kissed her deeply.

Julia vaguely heard Steve's voice call for champagne for everyone as she placed one of the rings on Carmen's finger and then offered her own shaking hand for her to do the same. Her heart overflowed with love and she wanted to shout it from the roof tops.

She said yes!

Steve stood and took the microphone Quinn brought to their table. "I've seen many couples come together in this town. Hell, I've even helped a few along the way."

Laughter erupted again throughout the hall but died down to silence. All waited for him to continue.

"But I have to say this is the first time I've been taken completely by surprise. I bet Brigid and Miranda it would take a few more days before Julia popped the question." His eyes appeared to twinkle and dance in the lights of the concert hall, mesmerizing Julia a bit as he waited for another round of laughter to fade away. "And don't you think for one minute, I won't be earning back the money I lost to those women with the artwork Julia's agreed to create for my casinos. All joking aside though, I want to give you both the wedding of your dreams. Whenever and wherever you wish to get hitched, it's on me."

Carmen shook her head. "That's very gracious of you but—"

Steve raised an eyebrow and looked to Jacob and Quinn for a little help.

However, Eric once again chimed in., "You're a part of the family now, Doc. There's no use arguing with him about it. When he makes up his mind, there's nothing changing it back."

Carmen laughed and put her hands up in mock surrender. "Okay, okay! I see I'm outnumbered here. You've got yourself a deal." She looked to Julia for her vote. "That is if it's what you want too."

"I've already got everything I ever wanted the moment you said yes. I'm going to take the advice Eric gave me when I first got to this town. I can't control everything that will or won't happen, so there's no use trying to fight it. Let's just go with it, Carmen. It is Vegas after all."

* * * *

Chapter 31

Eleven months later, Quebec City, Canada

Julia laughed again, recalling the look on Steve's face when they told him they wanted to be married in the chapel at the Ice Hotel in Canada. He must have been sure they would choose something a bit more warm and cozy, like Hawaii or even Australia. After they told him what they envisioned, he seemed to be all for it. Of course he needed to be sure everything met with their specifications, even going as far as commissioning the design of the famous resort. Steve told them he would give them a wedding they'd never forget, and boy did he ever follow through.

Theirs would be the first wedding of the year, since the hotel is only open for guests and tours from January through April. It'd disappointed Carmen slightly, as she hoped for a Christmas themed wedding in December. Unfortunately, it'd been the exact same time when a new hotel of ice by tradition must be created from scratch every year, so their initial plans were a wash. After seeing the first photographs of what the ice sculpting crews did to create the winter wonderland of her dreams, all doubts faded from her mind.

Now here they were about to have their fairy tale Christmas wedding in January.

Arriving three days before their nuptials were to take place, Julia and Carmen were able to get settled into their suite at the Four Points by Sheraton. Then they made the half hour ride to the Hotel de Glace. As soon as she walked into the foyer of the Ice Bar, she gasped in surprise.

The intricate details in all the carvings and sculptures covering the walls, the twinkling ice chandeliers, and the dizzying height of the vaulted ceilings would've bedazzled anyone. "So? Will this do?" Steve startled her just a bit as he entered the room behind her. "I mean, if this isn't what you had in mind, I'm sure we can postpone—"

"Don't you dare! This is so much more than we ever dreamed. I have to say you've really outdone yourself, Mr. Eischer. I don't know how I'll ever be able to repay you for all of this." She turned and buried her face into his parka, hiding the tears she knew were threatening to spill over yet again.

The last month seemed like a whirlwind of activity while finishing up all the details for the wedding. She nearly experienced a nervous breakdown, trying to make sure everything turned out perfectly. It'd been Steve who slowed her down and helped her to relax. Well—him and a couple nights getting flat out drunk on tequila shots at Saints and Sinners. Besides Carmen, she'd never known someone who she could honestly call a friend, but over the last year, Steve indeed became more than just her boss.

"Hey, now. I just left Carmen in tears in the chapel with Quinn and Jake. I don't think I can handle both of you all weepy eyed at the same time." He patted her on the back. "I told you a long time ago this is the sort of thing I do for my family and like it or not, you and Carm are a part of it. I don't expect repayment, other than the smiles on your faces. Got that?"

She lifted her head from his chest, and paused as he wiped the tears from her cheeks. "I got it. You know I'm still trying to wrap my mind around being part of all this. Besides my grandmother, none of my blood relatives ever cared whether I lived or died. Now I'm part of not only one, but two huge families, all because of Jake and Quinn. Carmen isn't close to any of her relatives either, so you're all we have. All of you've gone out of your way to make our day extra special. This is just so much more than I've ever imagined. Thank you."

"It's my pleasure, darlin'. Come on. Let's get a look at where Brigid will pronounce you and Carm spouses for life. You won't believe how the ice behind the altar is etched to make it look like stained glass."

"Oh! I forgot to make sure she can legally marry us here. I mean sure, she's a Wiccan priestess and all, but will Canada recognize her credentials?"

Steve's laughter echoed off the ice walls. "The moment the two of you asked her to do it, she made a few calls and she became ordained the very next day. She can perform weddings all over the States and Canada now. Relax. Everything is all set and ready for your big day."

"Hold it right there you two!" Quinn's voice rang out as they entered the chapel arm and arm. "I need to get the camera ready, so we can capture the look on Julia's face as she sees all of this for the first time."

Steve reached into his pocket and pulled out a monogrammed handkerchief. "You're gonna need this and afterwards, we're all gonna need a few shots of vodka at the Ice Bar!"

* * * *

Usually, there would only be a violinist to accompany the bridal party as they walked across the red carpet, past the ice benches covered with deer skins and filled with guests. Today, however, Derek played the acoustic guitar while Brigid and Quinn sang one of Julia's favorite songs by Melissa Etheridge.

"My intentions are true, won't you take me with you..."

The haunting words touched her deeply and were the perfect choice for their wedding song. Julia made her way down toward the woman who held her heart now, forever and always.

The brides both chose similar off white gowns edged in fur with matching hooded capes.

Carmen wore her hair up, using the jade clip from Maui.

Julia added a few curls to her short hair and wore the jade earrings Carmen gave to her the night before.

Both were adorned with beautiful jade and diamond pendants, gifts from the Hartley and Quartermarsh families.

Everyone's eyes were upon her but Julia focused only on Carmen's face as she walked, holding onto Steve's arm for dear life. All the other guests in their formal wear, covered in capes and furs to keep warm, soon faded away. The only one who mattered stood there, waiting for her with open arms.

Brigid stepped up behind altar and asked them to join hands, right to right, and left to left. While they did, she loosely tied a braided cord in a figure eight around their crossed wrists using six knots.

Carmen smiled and squeezed her hands as the cord bound them together.

Julia's vision swam a bit as fresh tears filled her eyes. She held Carmen's hands tighter and prayed she didn't do anything to embarrass herself like pass out in front of everyone.

"Julia and Carmen have come here today to proclaim their love and to pledge their heart and souls to one another in front of family and friends. The joining of their hands in this manner, is called a hand fasting and it's a tradition of old. It's a joining of two souls, binding them together through each and every life time. It's a way for them to find each other again, as their bond can never be broken. The tying of the cord six times is also symbolic as six is the number of love. It's the love between Julia and Carmen that's kept them together all these years, through triumph and despair, through their darkest hours, and now their brightest days. They will open their hearts to each other and forever join them, never allowing anything or anyone to tear apart the bond they make today. Will you all pledge to watch over their union and help them keep their bond safe?"

Voices of all in attendance then answered, "Aye!"

"Now our couple would like to recite a poem together they feel tells their story as well as that of many lovers who were lost and then found each other again." Brigid nodded to Carmen to begin to first lines of the poem called 'Safe Harbor.'

Carmen squeezed Julia's hands tightly before she began her lines. "You are the song my heart beats to, a rhythm wild and free. You give me purpose again, opened my eyes to see the goddess in me."

Julia felt the tears fill her eyes as she nearly missed her cue. "You lift me up higher than I could have ever dreamed of reaching alone. With you by my side, I can do anything, get through any adversity, and celebrate every joy. You are the safe harbor and the light that guides me home."

"Your love anchors me enough so I can soar wild and free, and yet still be safe in your arms at night. Your strength and courage are beacons bright and true, encouraging me to do what's right."

Now the tears were falling freely down both of their cheeks and Julia needed to swallow a few times before she could finish. "There was a time not so long ago when I thought all hope was lost, and I could go on no longer. Your heart kept calling out to me. Your love always lighting the way back to you, my heart, my soul, my safe harbor."

Brigid slipped the knotted cords from their hands and placed it into a beautifully carved wooden box. "I've placed the symbol of your union in this box, locking it to keep it safe. Each of you holds a key and can open it at any time when you need a reminder of all you pledge here today. We are not perfect creatures, so there will be moments when you need to recall your vows and promises you make today. Forever is not just for the happy times, but the deep dark ones as well. You've already shown you can accept each other during those times. This box is just to keep you centered." She then picked up two silver chalices filled with wine. "Julia, your cup is filled with red and Carmen has chosen the white. The red symbolizes the deep and undying love and passion you have for each other and the white for the purity of your bond and the love that's destined to be for all time."

Carmen poured some of her wine into Julia's chalice. "Beloved, I share with you the ocean of my heart, the rivers of my woman's body and the sweetness of my dreams. This is my wedding gift to you."

Julia in turn poured some of the mixed wine back into Carmen's cup and repeated the same verse. They both poured the wine back and forth four more times, then completed their lines together. "May our love be bound and witnessed by she who is eternal in the body of Mother Earth beneath our feet."

"Julia and Carmen do you promise to work as partners, to love honor and respect each other, to hold each other in your hearts, and stay with each other through struggles and pleasures all the days of your life and beyond?"

"We do."

Brigid smiled brightly. "This is my favorite part. By the powers bestowed upon me by The Three and the beautiful providence of Quebec, I pronounce you spouses now, forever, and always. Go ahead. Kiss your bride and make it official!"

Their guests applauded and cheered as Julia melted into Carmen's arms. This was the place she longed to be all her life. Finally, no more fighting to keep her secrets buried. No more having to protect the innocent little girl from the monsters.

At last, she could break down what remained of the walls surrounding her heart and just surrender.

THE END

About the Author

As the founder of Sassy Vixen Publishing, Tammy has a lot on her plate. Not only has she established herself as an erotic romance author with Siren Bookstrand, but she's also published two books of poetry and has many more projects underway. Finding time to write and keep up a full schedule as a veterinarian in a very busy practice in the Pacific Northwest has been a difficult task, but one she takes on happily with the help of her husband, "Mr. Vixen."

Through her website/blog Behind Closed Doors and her blog Not Enough Time in the Day you can get a glimpse into her hectic schedule. Now she can add Best Selling Author to her resume as her vampire inspired poetry book ***The Courtship of the Vampyre*** is one of the top sellers on Omnilit (ARe affiliate).

The love of books of all genres helped her decide to write under four pen names. This way she's able to tell the stories all of her characters wish to tell whether it's the sweet and sensual or hot and spicy. Speaking of spicy, Tammy is also part of the Four Seduced Muses along with three of her Siren author friends. No topic is off limits with the Muses and that's the way "The Vixen" likes it!

Readers can also connect with her and her alter egos through Facebook and Twitter.

www.ingramcontent.com/pod-product-compliance
Lightning Source LLC
La Vergne TN
LVHW091144080826
845145LV00008B/2247

* 9 7 8 0 9 9 1 3 8 3 6 1 0 *